B.C.CHASE
Pluto's Ghost

B.C. CHASE is the internationally bestselling author of the *Paradeisia Trilogy* which critics have hailed as "one of the greatest franchises of our time." His electrifying talent for combining the latest in scientific breakthroughs with edge-of-your-seat thrills has earned him a reputation as a master of suspense. Amazon has ranked him #1 in Religion and Spirituality, among its top ten Sci-fi authors, and a top 20 writer of Thrillers.

"B.C. CHASE IS RAPIDLY BECOMING AN AUTHOR OF AUTHORITY."
GRADY HARP, VINE VOICE

"CHASE HAS MASTERED THE ART OF WRITING SUSPENSE."
L.A. HOWELL

"IN TRUE CRICHTON STYLE, CHASE TAKES ELEMENTS OF KNOWN SCIENCE, EXPLORES THEIR EXTREME POTENTIAL, AND BUILDS A MYSTERY AROUND SCIENTIFIC PRINCIPLES."
-AMAZON.COM

"CHASE HAS TALENT YOU WON'T SOON FORGET."
-AMAZON.COM

"CHASE IS A BRILLIANT WRITER WITH A BOATLOAD OF TALENT."
-VINCENT VERITAS

"CHASE KEEPS YOU WANTING MORE."
-DEBRA HANSEN

Visit bcchase.com for free book offers.

Also by B.C.CHASE:

Leviathan
Glass
Paradeisia: Origin of Paradise
Paradeisia: Violation of Paradise
Paradeisia: Fall of Paradise
Cataton

*Epub.us

Copyright © 2017 B.C.CHASE

No part of this book may be used or reproduced in any manner whatsoever without written permission except in the case of brief quotations embodied in critical articles and reviews.

Preseption Press

ISBN: 978-1977718365

This is a work of fiction. Corporations, characters, organizations, or other entities in this novel are the product of the author's imagination, or, if real, are used fictitiously without any intent to describe their actual conduct.

Visit bcchase.com for free book offers.

This volume contains a bonus preview of *Paradeisia: Origin of Paradise.*

Table of Contents

One 17

Two 22

Three 25

Four 34

Five 41

Six 50

Seven 56

Eight 62

Nine 71

Ten 80

Eleven 85

Twelve 92

Thirteen 99

Fourteen 107

Fifteen 115

Sixteen 119

Seventeen 124

Eighteen 131

Nineteen 137

Twenty 145

Twenty-one 151

Twenty-two 155

Twenty-three	161
Twenty-four	168
Twenty-five	172
Twenty-six	178
Twenty-seven	183
Twenty-eight	186
Twenty-nine	190
Thirty	194
Thirty-One	200
Thirty-Two	204
Thirty-three	209
Preview of Paradeisia: Origin of Paradise	211
A Note from the Author	217
FAQ	**Error! Bookmark not defined.**
Glossary of Abbreviations and Technical Terms	219
Selected References	**Error! Bookmark not defined.**

This volume contains a bonus preview of *Paradeisia: Origin of Paradise.*

16

One

I'm unemployed. I'm seventy-five years old. I hate flying. But I'm sitting on 90,000 gallons of kerosene about to be blasted into space on a mission that cost four hundred billion bucks.

Go figure.

NASA told me that I should wear my helmet on the way up. I said, "No, thanks." I know that helmet or no helmet, if we're dumped on the ocean, it will be as fine ash. If they don't like it, they can kiss my saggy, old butt.

The date is May 18th, 2020. The time is 4:27 a.m.. The windows rim the top of the cockpit like holes at the top of an egg. The seats are in two rows: three closest to the nose and three behind. I'm positioned in the right rear (or, in spaceship speak, starboard aft). My back is to the ground in a seat that was clearly not designed by La-Z-Boy. Aside from three screens and a number of buttons and joysticks situated in the nose, the cabin is bare. The walls are dark gray and look like they are made of carbon fiber.

The suit I'm wearing doesn't look like much. It's puffy, wrinkled, and fluorescent orange like a highway cone. Why orange? So that if something goes wrong and we get dumped on the Atlantic, we can be rescued more easily. This tells me that the only thing you have to do to be hired by NASA for spacesuit design is display euphoric optimism during your interview. "Mr. Perkins, what do you think your chances of winning the lottery are, this year?"

"About a hundred percent."

"Perfect. You're just the kind of person we're looking for. You'll be making this year's space suits."

The screens show buttons, numbers, graphs, and geometric shapes. I don't have a clue what any of the buttons are for or what any of the shapes mean. They tried to teach me in case of an emergency, but I told 'em if I was going to die in space, I wanted to die sitting peacefully, twiddling my thumbs. Anyway, it's not as if I would be the one to save us should something go wrong. That would be up to one of the other members of the crew: highly esteemed and capable astronauts who spent much of their lives preparing for this. Now, they are busy jabbering with Houston—all the preflight mumbo-jumbo, but during flight prep, when we were being suited up and doing the pressure tests and all that, I was surprised to see they looked like they were anxious. They were wringing their hands and their eyes were open wide like cattle. I guess in the end we're all just human beings and, training or not, knowing that the chances of death within the next thirty minutes are about one in nine is enough to make anybody a little nervous.

On the list of top candidates, I would probably fit somewhere between six and seven billion. As I said, I don't have any qualifications to be here. I used to listen to science audiobooks in my rig, but that's as far as my interest in science goes. (You have to listen to something when you're on the road for five hundred miles a day.) In fact, about the only things that qualify me to go to space at all is that I have traveled more miles than anyone here except for our commander and I am the only one to live in something with an APU. Through my years as a trucker, I logged over five million miles. That's a far cry from the five *billion* or so miles it will take us to reach Pluto, but if I had driven my trucks to the moon instead of all over America, I could have made about ten round trips. So take that, Commander Tomlinson.

Commander Josh Tomlinson is thirty years old. To me, his face has a child-like quality, but since he is less than half my age, I suppose that shouldn't be surprising. His eyes are large and brown, his cheeks full, and his hair curly. You might think that, being so young, he would lack self-confidence and assurance, but nothing could be further from the truth. It is obvious that he does not have the slightest doubt about the correctness of everything he says and does. That clearly cannot come from experience, given his age, so I assume it comes from his natural intelligence. As far as raw smarts and quick wits go, I suspect few could match him. His technical knowledge—in fact his knowledge in general—is genius-level. He doesn't seem to care if any of us like him, and is obsessed with his business. I like that because his business is getting us to Pluto *safely*. Not sure how much I want to go to Pluto, but since that's where we're going, I want it to be a safe trip.

A *safe trip*. From everything I've heard, that's an oxymoron in this case. There's nothing about this trip that is safe. And, to make things worse, if we do meet our doom, in all likelihood it won't be a quick and easy passing. What I said earlier about being dumped on the Atlantic as a fine ash is technically not accurate. All the bodies from the Challenger disaster were recovered (from their seats in the crew cabin) and plenty of the remains from Columbia were found. NASA made me watch the video of Columbia's last moments before it ripped up, and they showed me pictures of the body parts. They said they wanted me to be fully aware of the risks (translation: we're trying to scare you out of going because we'd prefer someone else). In the video, the crew are joking and having a good time, passing around the camera, and admiring the view of the billowing plasma outside the windows. Then the video goes dead, and what you don't see is the cockpit spiraling out of control, the pilot flipping switches, astronauts frantically putting on their helmets and gloves, the cabin depressurizing, and their bodies breaking free from the seat restraints as the vehicle spins faster than a blender. I'm trying not to think about that. As you can see, I'm having a tough time keeping it out of my mind.

Out of the prelaunch blabber, something over the radio from Houston catches my ear, "And tell Jim he still needs to put his helmet on."

Commander Tomlinson turns his head and says, "Jim, you need to put your helmet on."

"Copy that," I say. "I don't know where it is."

Commander Tomlinson says, "He doesn't know where his helmet is."

Houston replies, "We found it. He left it down here with his brain."

I hear chuckles all over the radio.

By the time we reach Pluto, the communications delay will be nine hours roundtrip. If we were to have a serious medical emergency, whoever needed help would probably be dead by the time we heard back from the flight surgeon in Houston. For this reason, and the fact that it just makes us all feel better, we have our own personal doctor: Shelby Montana, thirty-one, from Louisiana. I think it's safe to say she's the favorite member of the crew. She spent most of her medical career as an emergency room doctor. Does that mean NASA is expecting us to have a lot of emergencies? I don't know, but I do know she has also been getting a lot of time in practicing common surgeries. She has poofy hair (which I assume will only get poofier once we reach outer space), bright, bunny-like eyes, and a small mouth with two big front teeth that she happily exposes when she smiles and laughs—and she smiles and laughs a lot. She's kind of like our mother hen—clucking at us and pestering us with admonitions about our health and diet all the time. Like a caring mother, we wouldn't want to do without her even if she can be a little irritating. She does it because she cares. She's also the one who pulls you aside for a heart-to-heart if she senses you aren't perfectly happy, and her senses are as sharp as a hound's.

The psychologist on this mission is Shiro Nakamura, forty-two, from Japan. He will keep an eye on our mental wellbeing, but I think his presence here has more to do with the purpose of our mission. He's also a linguist. He has brown eyes and a generally severe expression. He's very open-minded, but once he has formed his opinion, you could move a mountain more easily than you could persuade him that he's wrong.

Also aboard are the lovebirds of the mission: Timothy Manning, thirty-four, from Ireland and Doctor Nari Park, twenty-seven, from South Korea. They're married, though at times it's hard to tell if they love space more or each other. Tim is our pilot. The computer will be doing most of the flying, so he will also be responsible for maintenance. He's a stellar programmer, from what I'm told. Nari is one of our "mission specialists" (also what they're calling me, though I don't specialize in anything). She is a biologist. They're both optimistic, easy-going characters. Tim is blonde and has an unimpeachable smile, big dimples, and ears that flash red when he's embarrassed or laughing. Nari has long, jet-black hair which she keeps in a ponytail, a narrow chin, and big, round eyes.

The cabin is starting to vibrate and I hear a rushing sound like a giant toilet flushing. That's the fuel. Now the cabin shakes and a deep roar reverberates from under us. The engines have fired. This is it. I can't turn back now. I can't raise my hand and say, "I changed my mind. I want to get off." I'm going to space. Pluto, here I come.

Two

I look over at the kids sitting next to me: Shelby and Tim and Nari. (I call them kids because they're so much younger than I am.) Shelby is staring straight up with a pleasant grin. Tim has the broadest smile you've ever seen and is holding Nari's hand. Nari seems almost as excited as he is, though she's more subdued because she's just not as gregarious as he is. He sees me looking at him and gives me the thumbs up.

I can feel all the blood drain from my head. My mind is a whirlwind of thoughts:

"Jim, you idiot."

"Jim, you idiot."

"Jim, you idiot."

Yes, that's my name. Jim. Jim Perkins, the truck driver who is going to Pluto.

Well, I suppose *they* have a reason for choosing me. Out of all the billions of people on this small, blue ball, Jim Perkins's name showed up. NASA has puzzled over it ever since the list came through. But nothing stood out. Not my biology. Certainly not my brains: the most education I have is a high school diploma. I'm just your average, ordinary, run-of-the-mill person with nothing to recommend me.

Maybe that's why I accepted the invite: because I was *chosen*. See, I used to be the one who makes all the choices. I chose all my dates for high school proms. I chose to be team captain in football. I chose to be student body president. I chose to go on the fast track to success by skipping college. I chose to start trucking. I chose to marry the girl of my dreams. I chose to make love to my new bride (and about a year later my daughter was born). I chose to divorce my wife after she made love to someone else. I chose to buy a house out in the country with acreage and a pond. I chose to leave trucking after a truck crushed my daughter's car between it and another semi, rolling the roof off like a can of sardines. So it's nice to have somebody else do the choosing, for once. They chose *me* for this mission and, to be frank, I guess I'm flattered, so I'm going.

Who is *they*? They're not UFO's, mind you. People in the press have been calling them UFO's a lot, but that's a misnomer. We have never seen them, we don't know if they fly, and they're awfully smart for being mere objects. They would better be called "Unidentified Galactic Intelligences." One thing we do know about them is that they were at least 140 astronomical units away. That's about thirteen billion miles. We know that because that's how far Voyager 1 was when it—well wait, I'm getting ahead of myself.

I'll never forget that phone call (never being a rather insignificant period because it's likely I'll die in the next few minutes on my way through the stratosphere). I was laying on the bed of my rig, getting some shuteye, when my cell phone rang. The cab of my semi-truck is actually pretty spacious, with a twin-sized bed, a refrigerator, a microwave, and lots of storage space. For some people, the noise of the APU (that's the auxiliary power unit that provides a/c) could be a bit much, but I always found it to be sleep-inducing. (Or maybe that was the fourteen hours I had spent on the road.)

I pulled the phone from its pouch beside my bed. It's an old clamshell phone. Doesn't do anything fancy like the ones everybody's always got an inch or two from their faces, these days. Squinting at the digital screen, I didn't recognize the caller ID, so I pushed the big red button on the keypad. It rang again. I dismissed it again. It rang a third time. I answered it. "It's three o'clock in the morning," I growled. "Who is this?"

"This is John Hogarth, the administrator of NASA."

So there I was, on the bunk of my truck at three o'clock in the morning with a phone to my ear and the administrator of the National Aeronautics and Space Administration on the other end of the line.

"Do you know why I am calling you, Mr. Perkins?"

"Is this about those fireworks I shot off July 4th? Honest, I had no idea they would go that high."

Crickets.

I cleared my throat, "No, I don't know why you're calling me."

"Mr. Perkins, you won a free trip to visit the Jet Propulsion Laboratory. Congratulations."

Now that was a head-scratcher. I had no recollection of entering a contest for a free trip to NASA.

"Are you at home?"

"I'm a trucker. I'm on the road." Now I was suspicious. "Who did you say you are again?"

"I am John Hogarth, the administrator of NASA. I report to the President of the United States of America. Where are you, now?"

"I'm at the Big D truck stop off highway ninety-five at exit 104."

"We will send a helicopter to pick you up."

"Now?"

"Yes, now."

I decided to play along, expecting that I would be asked for my bank account information so they could send me my winnings or something. I said, "Okay, I'm driving a blue Freightliner Cascadia license number 23826. There's room for a helicopter behind me, just watch out for trucks coming in and out."

"Perfect. You can expect the helicopter in about an hour," Hogarth said, and hung up.

Three

I feel like an ant sitting on top of one of those machines that jiggle away your fat. The extreme vibration and the sound of the thunder beneath us—like a thousand sonic booms a minute—are reminders of how much we are at the mercy of the giant engines we are riding. Even louder than the engines, though, is the wind. It sounds like a freight train. The cabin is rattling, with creaks coming from all over, and our seats don't seem to be that securely fastened to the floor as they're shaking all over.

Commander Tomlinson is keeping his hands close to his chest—presumably so he doesn't accidentally poke one of the touch screens. He looks relaxed, but his voice is strained over the radio. He says, "There are the clouds at 20,000." The black sky briefly brightens through the windows.

Suddenly, an alarm sounds.

"What do we got, Shelby?" Commander Tomlinson asks.

"DP/DT is about point zero seven," Shelby strains to say.

Houston asks, "In the positive or negative?"

"Negative," she replies.

"No action on DP/DT," Houston says.

"Gotcha," Shelby says.

"You ready for four *G*'s, Perkins?" Tim asks.

I reply, "Four *G*'s? I could have sworn we were already doing ten."

Tim laughs ironically, "Not remotely."

Commander Tomlinson says, "Stage one cutoff in five seconds."

"Confirm stage one cutoff," Houston says.

There is a sudden jolt.

"Stage two start," Commander Tomlinson says.

"Stage two start," confirms Houston.

Another jolt and I feel like I'm on a roller coaster, but there isn't as much rumble from the engines because we've come high enough that the atmosphere is thin.

After a few moments, Houston tells us we can open our visors. Since I didn't wear my helmet, I have no visor to open.

I can sense that the cabin is shifting. I feel kind of like I'm upside down, though the engines are still pressing me back against my seat. A curved line of orange appears through the upmost windows. It grows stronger like the spark of a long flame in the blackness. I see a sliver of light at the edge of the lowest window to the right. I realize I am looking at the moon, a crescent of silver below us in a sea of black. We are definitely upside down. Another bright pin of light appears to the left. It is remarkably quiet. I can barely hear the rumble of the engine anymore.

Shelby nudges me, "That's Venus, our first destination. You'll see Mercury next." And, sure enough, I see another, smaller pin of light.

A spot of rainbow-rimmed light appears on the floor of the cabin. The light shifts as the cabin tilts until a flood of light gushes in, unbridled and crystalline. The sun blazes, clear and vibrant, directly in front of us. Above us is the edge of earth's horizon, beautiful and blue with sunlight glowing golden at its edge and streaming through tiny clouds on its surface. The sight takes my breath away.

Commander Tomlinson says, "It's beautiful up here, Houston."

"Beautiful," Shelby repeats, gazing in awe.

The sun continues to lower under the horizon, a beacon of brilliance hanging in the dark. Commander Tomlinson says, "Stage two cutoff ten seconds."

"Confirm stage two cutoff," Houston echoes.

And, suddenly, the pressure pushing me back against my seat stops. I feel like I'm falling. I grip the edges of my seat. The feeling of falling won't stop. Blood is rushing to my head. I'm starting to panic. But then, the falling sensation dissipates and I feel a little dizzy and start to black out. Someone's hand is moving into my field of vision. The hand moves slowly and I see that it isn't attached to any arm. Someone's hand has been chopped off and the hand is floating towards my face. *Oh, gosh*, I think. It's happening. We've had an accident. Blackness is closing in.

"Jim?" Shelby's voice says. "Jim? Are you okay?" She gently pats my cheek.

I take a deep breath and my vision returns. She has left her seat and is in front of me. The hand was not a hand at all. It is her glove. Her feet are not planted on the floor where they should be. She's floating.

"Welcome to space," Commander Tomlinson says, looking at me from behind Shelby.

With an especially wide smile—even for him—Tim says, "A lot better than four G's, isn't it?"

I lift my hands and tap Shelby's glove. It drifts before my face. I push it back and forth between my hands. I look at Tim and smile, probably appearing like a seventy-five-year-old child. "I like it!" I giddily exclaim. I suppose it's a good thing I wasn't the first man on the moon because that would have been an unfortunate choice of words for Armstrong when he stepped out of the lunar module, no matter how sincerely he uttered them.

Shelby is passing around water bags that have straws with valves on them. I want to try some mid-air summersaults, but she wants me to worry about hydration. I protest, "I'm not thirsty."

She questions, "Did you drink that soda before we left? I told you not to do that!"

"I had to have my last Coke!"

She shakes her head, "It's a wonder anyone from your generation lives past fifty-five."

First order of business once we are hydrated is to get these bulky spacesuits off. Underneath the suits we are wearing nothing fancy: just t-shirts and khaki pants or, in my case, loose-fitting Wranglers. It takes us a good thirty minutes to disrobe, a task made a little tricky by the fact that the interior of the Origins capsule is a mere eleven feet across at its widest point. Once the suits have been stowed, the crew start reviewing their post-launch checklist.

What do *I* have to do? Hope and pray I can hold my bladder, because, although I'm wearing a MAG (that's an astronaut diaper), I am determined not to use it. Everyone assured me it was no big deal, that it's expected we will fill our diapers during or after launch. Maybe it's because I'm closer than these kids to that stage of life when diapers could become a routine part of my get-up, but for whatever reason I simply won't use my diaper. I just won't. It's going to be a big challenge not to because we will be stuck in here for six hours while we perform a Hohmann transfer and get our spacecraft aligned with the space station.

First, I watch Commander Tomlinson lead the crew through their checklist, but that quickly gets boring, so I decide to get a closer look at earth from 400,000 feet through the windows. If you ever imagined what it might be like to see earth from space, let me assure you your imagination cannot possibly do it justice. As I gaze out, I stop breathing. The deep black of space is contrasted sharply by the blue radiance of our planet. I watch in awe while we pass over the glinting ocean sunrise, the tops of the billowing clouds catching the orange light of the sun. I see a green coast approaching and my mind struggles to make geographic sense of it. I see one landmass edged on top by another long and almost crescent-like mass. Some other form is behind these, but I have no idea what it is or what I'm looking at. Tim comes beside me and peers out. He smiles, "There's my home."

"*That's* Ireland?"

"And England and Scotland, yes."

It doesn't look like the Ireland and England I'm used to seeing on maps, at all. From here, they look gigantic, like continents. Yet, within two minutes, we've passed over the United Kingdom and we're heading over France and Belgium. Tim returns to his tasks, but I keep watching.

By the time the International Space Station slips into view above us, we have been all the way around the earth four times.

To me, the six hours have passed like minutes. Below the ISS, a space shuttle is visible, floating over the serene backdrop of clouds and ocean with its cargo bay doors spread open. The shuttle's nose is raising very slowly, revealing the word Atlantis on its starboard wing.

Commander Tomlinson peers out the window next to me. To the rest of the crew, he says, "She's doing the RPM. A waste of time. I still can't believe they chose to dig up the dumb, old shuttles."

For me, someone who saw the shuttles on television back when they were the pride of America's space program and unequalled in the world, the moment is powerful. They were never supposed to fly again, but Space Shuttle Atlantis floats before me in the vast beauty of space, a relic from more audacious times. Due to the accidents of Columbia and Challenger, and because of the prohibitive expense of launching them (between two hundred million and a billion per launch, depending upon how you calculate it), they were placed in exhibits at museums all over the country. Now, Atlantis, Discovery, Endeavor, and even Enterprise (which was not previously used in space) have performed a total of almost 150 missions in the span of two years—an unbelievable feat considering they had previously flown 135 missions in thirty years.

While, on the whole it was a remarkable success, it wasn't without tragedy. Discovery was lost last month when it exploded during the jettison of the SRBs. Seven crewmembers died.

The Shuttle Program was originally designed to fly as many as 180 missions a year, with a two-week prep time for each shuttle. Conceived to be like an airliner, reusable and with a speedy relaunch, NASA sold the program on what turned out to be wildly optimistic cost control. In practice, because the safety of each critical component had to be assured for every flight, the fastest turnaround record was set by Atlantis—at a whopping fifty-four days. This could have been much faster, but speed came at a tremendous price in terms of manpower, and as the public lost interest in the space program, budgets dwindled and NASA was forced to make do. With both the Challenger and Columbia disasters, additional safety protocols were put in place which further extended the time to launch. The net effect was a bloated program of low efficiency, ballooning expenditure, tragic failures, and seemingly endless delays.

Despite its big-time deficiencies, however, it was a program that had successfully built the ISS, a nearly million-pound behemoth with the interior volume of a five-bedroom house. Commander Tomlinson was in the meeting where Administrator Hogarth made the reluctant decision to bring the shuttles out of retirement. Tomlinson told us it was a very heated debate, with the shuttles receiving a lot of scorn from those (including Tomlinson himself) who saw them as fundamentally flawed, experimental aircraft that had failed and, with good reason, were put to rest. But in the end, it came down to the fact that, even with all the world's biggest rockets working overtime, only about half the heavy-lift launches NASA needed to complete the retrofit could be found. The space shuttle was the only vehicle available that could get the job done as quickly as it was needed, and for this mission, money was no object.

The shuttle is performing a slow backflip over the blue backdrop.

There are some loud noises as the thrusters are automatically fired in quick succession by the computer. A voice comes over the radio, "Station this is Houston for Origins. Confirm 250 meter hold for step two in one decimal one zero two."

A different voice responded, "Houston we confirm we have good range and corridor is displayed. It's looking good from our perspective."

"Okay we copy, thanks."

"Houston this is Station are you guys ready for block bravo?"

"Confirm block bravo."

I realize now that I really have to pee, and I'm still determined not to use the diaper I'm wearing, so I am relieved to hear this chatter. "How long 'till we can dock?" I ask.

My heart sinks when Commander Tomlinson replies, "About three hours. We have to wait for Atlantis."

Whereas before, six hours seemed like minutes, the hours to docking pass like a slow drip from a leaky faucet, and it's all I can do to keep my legs from dancing around. Finally, I lose control and I feel the warmth saturate my diaper. It's a surprisingly pleasant sensation, like dipping into a warm bath. As soon as I'm able, I stop the flow, determined to cling to at least a little bit of my dignity.

Atlantis finishes its backflip and then rises with its back to the forward-most point of the station. I stare in impatience as it makes excruciatingly slow progress in docking. Finally, I hear someone say, "Atlantis docked successfully. Beginning pressurization."

Atlantis is docked, now it's our turn. Ever so slowly, our Origins capsule rises up towards the underside of the space station. Our craft needs to get close enough that one of the station's robotic arms can capture us and reel us up to the node.

The station is impressively long (about the length of two football fields) and much larger than it used to be. The one hundred fifty post-retirement shuttle missions, in conjunction with another 170 additional missions performed by Atlas IV's, Atlas V's, Delta IV, Ariane V, H2, Falcon 9's, Falcon Heavy's, Proton's, and the ever-reliable Soyuz, have quadrupled the interior volume of the ISS. In addition to the fourteen sections it had before, it now has ten expandable Bigelow Aerospace B330 modules, each of which provide 514 square feet of space. These additions have been minor, however, compared to the structural trusses, thermal shields, rockets, and fuel tanks (spent space shuttle external tanks from all these construction missions) that have been retrofitted. The trusses have added the support that will be critical on a long-term voyage. The thermal shielding will protect us from the searing heat of the sun, and the rockets will power us away from the earth and towards our first target: Venus. Contained in a series of the massive titanium tanks at the aft end of the station is the fuel we will need for the journey to Pluto: over one million gallons of liquid oxygen, hydrogen, and hydrazine. The oxygen and hydrogen will get us out of earth orbit. The hydrazine, which can be stored almost indefinitely, will help us maneuver through space.

There is a clunking sound as the robotic arm attaches itself to our capsule, and I hear the astronauts congratulate one another on a successful capture. It takes minutes for the arm to swing us up into place under the same node that the shuttle is docked to. The capture is again a success, but instead of throwing open the hatch and rushing into the station to storm the bathroom, as I hoped to do, I find we must wait yet again for the compartment between the space station's hatch and our capsule's hatch to pressurize.

I've decided space is a lot like an amusement park: a lot of waiting for a few seconds of fun.

Finally, Commander Tomlinson rotates a crank lever on the hatch (in the front of our capsule behind the screens) and pulls inward. He passes through first, followed by Tim, then Nari, then Katia, then Shiro, then Shelby, and finally me.

Four

So-called "NASA Administrator John Hogarth" never asked for my bank account number. He hung up, and I thought to myself, "A prankster." I was just starting to doze off when the helicopter arrived. But it was so loud outside my truck that anybody who was in the parking lot could not possibly have slept through it. I quickly pulled on my jeans and slipped into a plaid shirt before jumping outside. There, with lights blinking and rotors spinning, blasting the pavement with wind and making the puddles shimmer, was a big helicopter. Don't ask me what kind it was because I don't know, but that it had come from the military was obvious, because it was large and green, like a big, fat bullfrog, and no commercial pilot in his right mind would operate a thing so ugly. A bunch of other truckers had sleepily emerged and were staring at the copter as if an alien spaceship had just landed.

I approached. Two soldiers jumped out and one of them asked me, "What is your name?"

"Jim Perkins."

"Come with us."

$$\Delta v \Delta v \Delta v \Delta v \Delta$$

I float through a narrow tunnel between two hatches and emerge into a brightly lit area about the size of a big, square room.

But it isn't anything like a room.

I am underneath a whole group of people whose sock-covered feet are right above my head. The "room" is very disorienting because on all sides (up, down, right, left, forward, backward) there are either square, gray hatches with little round windows or square openings with rounded corners on all sides. The hatches that have been open do not swing on hinges, but have been slid along grooves to be tucked neatly against the white walls.

The crew are greeting and hugging a surprisingly large number of people who are already on the station. I recognize a couple of them. One is Commander Eric Sykes, fifty-seven, from Boston. He is in charge of the Atlantis shuttle that docked before our Origins capsule did. They are dropping off the last shipment of material for one of the horticulture modules and will be taking a spacewalk to fix a jammed solar array that cannot be retracted. He is a famous astronaut, a veteran of the shuttle program who was called out of retirement. During training, he came in on many occasions to give us some experiential pointers. He is bald, has narrow-set eyes, wide jaws, and broad shoulders. He's a pretty serious character. Doesn't smile much except when the press or NASA are pointing cameras at him and he has no choice, and even then his smile isn't very pleasant. But he's sharp. I like him.

Commander Sykes spots me and floats down to shake my hand, "Jim, welcome to the ISS. Are you ready?"

"Ready as I'll ever be," I say. "Sure you don't want to join us?"

He gets a far-off look in his eyes as he says, "In a way, believe it or not, I do." He shakes his head, "But no. I've missed my family too much already."

"You hold the record for the American longest in space, don't you?"

He nods.

Jokingly, I say, "Well I'm glad they tested it out on the amateurs before the real astronauts like me came up." That gets a little grin out of him.

Swooping down to hug me is a young woman with large, green eyes and blonde hair which has been gathered into a top knot, "Welcome, Jimmy!" she exclaims. A trip to space wouldn't be complete without a cosmonaut, and she is ours: Katia Pavlova. She has already been on the station for a week (she came up on a Russian Soyuz spacecraft), but unlike the rest of the station crew, will be joining us to Pluto. We trained together and, during that time, she kind of adopted me as a substitute father. In addition to being the youngest member of the crew, she is probably also the smartest. At only twenty-two, she already has two PhDs, one in astrophysics and the other in mathematics. From what I've seen, she has all the best qualities of youth: energy, daring, and optimism, but little of the swagger or stupidity.

"The station is so big! I'm so excited!" she exclaims with a broad smile.

Commander Sykes introduces me to the other members of his shuttle crew. Three of them I have already met during my training at NASA. Sanjin Vidić, a chipper, thick-haired technical specialist from India, and Maria Vasquez, a middle-aged technical specialist from Mexico, are helping to do some last-minute work on the station to make it ready for flight. Both are experienced astronauts. Sarah Foreman, a gray-haired botanist who looks like she cares much more for plants than her own hairdo, is with them to make sure everything in the horticulture modules is ready for our long journey. Kurt Drexel I have not met. He is the shuttle pilot, from Germany. I will spend the next two days with them as the station is prepared to launch from LEO—that's a little lingo I picked up: low earth orbit.

The Station Commander is Viktor Filipchenko. He has bright, optimistic eyes and greets me warmly as if welcoming me to his home. I guess that shouldn't seem unusual since this has been his home for the last six months.

Having shaken everybody's hands, I tell Katia, "Where's the bathroom on this thing?"

"First, you need to know the basic directions. Zenith is up, nadir is down, starboard is the right side of the ship, port is the left side. Now follow me, the bathroom is this way—aft and to port."

Like a diver through water, she launches herself aft-ward. She says, "This module is called Node 2. We have workbenches in here, stowage, and the launch seats." We pass two metallic, blue tables that are folded against the wall. An assortment of the types of tools that would be found in any garage tool chest, pens, and duct tape are attached above the tables. Past these on all four sides are odd-looking blue seats with restraints and minimal padding. They look a bit like something you'd strap a person to before performing dental work on him.

We pass through a square entrance with round corners that leads to another module. In here the walls and ceiling are lined with all kinds of technical equipment: circular things, gray things with switches, wires running everywhere, metallic arms that hold laptops, displays with lists of numbers, tubes, two stations with joysticks, and an exercise bike. The floor is comprised of what appear to be stowage lockers. "This is the American Lab," she explains. "In here we have avionics computers, science material, and also this bike, for exercise." I am surprised to see how chaotic the place looks. The mockup space station on the ground where we did some of our training didn't look like this at all. To propel herself along, Katia uses blue rails that are affixed to the walls. I follow her example. She takes me through another entrance and into an area like the first one I entered with hatches and entrances on all sides. We float over a big cavity full of large, white parcels and bags to an area full of stained storage units in the walls and a red table. "This is Node 1. It's a nice place to prepare snacks, on this table. You can stick forks and things on here." She demonstrates how to use straps and Velcro pads on the table. She smiles, "But we have a bigger galley in the crew quarter module. If you want to know where the best food is hidden, ask me when you get hungry." She angles her body to turn to the right, where she passes through an entrance into another module. "Here is Node 3." She points to what looks like a conveyer belt recessed in the wall with a big bar. "The treadmill. You have to exercise at least two-and-a-half hours every day." Finally, much to my relief, she floats to a little enclosed space where, inside, I can see what is obviously a toilet, though it has a very tiny lid and, instead of porcelain, has a round, metal bottom. She loosens a strap to free a long tube with a yellow funnel at the end, topped by a cap. "You pee in this. It has suction. For the bigger stuff, take one of these baggies and stretch it over the toilet seat." She pulls a clear, plastic bag with elastic out from a holder on the wall. "When you're finished, wrap it up and push it down into the can." She shows me how to pull the screen closed so I can have privacy, and she leaves.

Of course, they had a mockup bathroom like this during training, but they just pointed to it and said, "That's the bathroom." Nobody actually showed us how to work it, so I'm mildly apprehensive about it.

I quickly discover there is nothing to be worried about. When a man is intimately acquainting himself with this kind of new equipment, his mind tends to wander. Mine wandered back to my first visit to JPL.

ΔvΔvΔvΔvΔ

After a transfer from the helicopter to a small jet on an airstrip in the middle of nowhere, I found myself riding in a van to NASA's Jet Propulsion Laboratory in California. I was brought to the Deep Space Network Control Room, which I found to be dark, with rows of workstations in front of a large display. Quiet and rather peaceful, it was just the kind of place you would expect to be communicating with all of our farthest-reaching space probes.

John Hogarth introduced himself. He was a tall man wearing a dress shirt, tie, and blue-patterned suit pants. Bald, he wore thin wire-framed glasses. He reached out to shake my hand, "Welcome to NASA."

"Thank you."

"How was your flight?"

"Very nice plane," I said, recalling the Gulfstream's plush leather chairs and the ample beverages that the gorgeous flight attendant served. "I could get used to that."

"I'm sure you could," he said, seriously, "but it's mine."

I raised my eyebrows, "Is the girl yours, too?"

He ignored my comment, saying, "You're probably wondering why you're here."

"Hey, as long as you keep up the good treatment, I won't ask any questions."

"Have you heard of the Voyager space probes, Voyager 1 and Voyager 2?"

"Don't ring a bell."

He said, "Everything I'm about to tell you must not leave this room. For now, this information is so sensitive, only the President, the Vice President, the Chief of Staff, and a handful of other people at NASA know about it. The President will stop at nothing to make sure this stays confidential."

"Pretty serious stuff, then?"

"Do you value your life, Mr. Perkins?"

"Who doesn't?"

"If you do, you'll keep this to yourself."

"Is this something I really want to know?"

"You have no choice, I'm afraid. None of us do."

"Got it. My lips are sealed."

He pensively surveyed me, as if he was having second thoughts. Then, he proceeded to tell me a about the history of Voyager 1. It was launched September 5th, 1977 on a mission to Jupiter, Saturn, and Titan—a fitting name for Saturn's biggest moon—and then off to the far reaches of our galaxy. Screwed onto the side was a "golden record" with a pulsar star map showing the solar system's location in the galaxy. Within the record were greetings in fifty languages, samples of music, pictures of earthlings, and two letters inviting the aliens to visit our humble planet: one from President Jimmy Carter and one from U.N. Secretary General Kurt Waldheim. Of course, the golden record was, in many people's minds, just a publicity grab by NASA to ensure a steady stream of funding. Few of the people there actually thought that aliens would ever discover it (with Carl Sagan being the notable exception).

On August 25th, 2012, Voyager 1 crossed into interstellar space. On March 1st, 2013, NASA received an unusual transmission from the spacecraft. At that time, Voyager was merely sending measurements from the sensors that had not been switched off to conserve power: a low energy charged particle instrument, a cosmic ray system, a plasma wave system, a triaxial fluxgate magnetometer, and so forth (I still don't know what any of those are). But this transmission was words.

He leaned over one of the workstations and told the person sitting there, "Charlie, can you please bring up the text of the message?"

Charlie, a guy with a mustache and glasses, said, "Sure, Mr. Hogarth." After a couple clicks, a single line of white words on a black background were displayed:

```
Hello. We received your record. Let's meet.
```

Five

Having learned some lessons about what *not* to do while taking care of the necessities in space, I open the accordion screen and exit the bathroom. I try to orient myself. I see the treadmill belt on the wall to the left and I hear voices coming from that direction, so I know which way to go. Before I leave the module, though, I notice a lot of bright light coming from a big entranceway in the floor. I dive down and find myself in a kind of a globe with seven windows. The view to the earth is somewhat obscured by large, round sections of the station, but it's still breathtaking.

Commander Tomlinson startles me from above, "Jim, what are you doing?"

The question irks me. *Can't he see what I'm doing?* I reply, "I'm trying to phone home."

"We have work to do. Come up out of there."

I push myself up and out of the "cupola," as I know it is called. Commander Tomlinson directs my attention to the outhouse, "You know what your job will be in this station, right?"

"Yeah, I think so."

"You'll be our housekeeper. I'll need you to keep all the bathrooms clean and stocked. You need to check these cans to see if they're full. Every six to eight weeks, they will be, and you'll need to seal them and take them to the horticulture modules."

"Ten-four, boss."

"I prefer 'yes, sir.' Come with me."

Commander Tomlinson leads me out of Node 3 to Node 1 where the food prep table, the food warmer, and the food packets are stored. He says, "You'll need to keep this, and all the other galleys, clean. Every time somebody opens something in here, a little bit of it is probably going to splatter on the walls. If you see it, clean it."

"Yes, sir," I say. Although I know NASA had little choice but to bring me along since I was on the aliens' official roster and, as such, there is little I could do to get kicked off the team, I want to be civil and respond as any of the other crew members would to an order from the commanding officer. If that means saying "yes, sir" to a kid half my age, then so be it. Still, he didn't treat me so condescendingly in training, and I'm kind of put off by the sudden shift in attitude. I speculate to myself that maybe he's feeling pressure to exhibit can-do leadership now that we're here on the station, so I'll let it slide. President Kennedy was given his first command when he was very young, and he quickly grew to fill the shoes. Probably this kid will do okay, too.

He leads me from here through the American Science Module with the exercise bike and the controller for one of the robotic arms. I am disoriented and can't tell what's up or down. Once we reach Node 2 (the place where we entered the station), he hangs a right, or starboard, into the European Science Module (which looks quite a bit like the American Science Module). He reaches up into a nook in the ceiling and pulls down a bag. "This is the vacuum cleaner. I'll let you know if I think you're not using it enough. Understood?"

"Yes, sir," I say, a big grin plastered on my face.

"Why are you smiling?

"I'm just relieved I brought my French maid outfit," I say. "That's all."

He isn't smiling. "Are we going to have a problem, Jim?"

"Nope, absolutely no problem, sir. Just trying to keep things light."

"This station is a 350-billion-dollar piece of equipment, and this mission couldn't be more important. Let's exhibit the respect and decorum that it deserves."

"Yes, sir."

"Now, come with me. Everybody went to check out the horticulture modules."

"It's pretty cute, if you want to see it."

ΔvΔvΔvΔvΔ

"They told us they wanted to meet on Pluto," Hogarth said. "They told us exactly when they wanted to meet. And, they sent us a list of who they wanted on our crew. You were the last person on that list."

Charlie brought up the list:

```
Josh Tomlinson: 30. Miami, Florida. Commander.
Shelby Montana: 31. Lafayette, Louisiana. Doctor.
Timothy Manning: 34. Dublin, Ireland. Pilot.
Shiro Nakamura: 36. Tokyo, Japan. Psychologist.
Nari Park: 27. Seoul, South Korea. Biologist.
Katia Pavlova: 22. St. Petersburg, Russia. Botanist.
Jim Perkins: 65. Wichita, Kansas. Truck driver.
```

Now that was a head-scratcher, right there. All those young scientists, and then me, the truck driver, tacked on the bottom. Left me thinking that either the aliens' typist made a blunder, or they're not too brainy.

Hogarth said, "All of these people were already astronauts when we received the list, except you. What do you think it is about you that would make them want you to come?"

"My natural-born charm?" I suggested.

"Mr. Perkins, this is a serious matter."

"Okay, okay. I don't know. I'm seventy-three years old, I drive a truck for a living, I live on a couple acres with a little fishing pond, and the only family I have is one daughter. There's nothing special about me. I'm just a nobody, Mr. Hogarth."

"Mr. Perkins, have you ever been contacted or been in contact with alien beings?"

I laughed, but stopped when I saw that he was getting irritated. "No, sir," I said.

"Have you ever tried to contact alien beings?"

"Nope. Well, I did talk to my mother-in-law a couple times, but I don't know if that counts."

Hogarth stared me in the eye for a minute, trying to judge my sincerity, I think. Then he said, "So you really don't know why they would choose you?"

"Nothing rings a bell."

"And we have no idea, either. To be frank, on a mission of this importance, we would rather send someone else."

"I can imagine," I said. "So, why don't you?"

"They insist that if we do not follow their instructions to the letter, there will be no one to meet us when we reach Pluto. That is an unacceptable risk to the President. He believes we must take this opportunity to have some control in the manner of first contact. In other words, if they are not here already, we don't want them here until we know as much about them as we can. Pluto is just about as far away as we could possibly get a human from earth given the technology we currently have."

"Why did *they* choose Pluto, though?"

"We have no idea," Hogarth replied. "You and Pluto are the two biggest puzzles about all of this. Pluto isn't even considered a planet, anymore."

"Pluto isn't even a planet, and I'm not even an astronaut," I grin. "A conundrum worthy of NASA's best scientists." I took a deep breath, and suggested, "Administrator Hogarth, if I were you, I wouldn't go anywhere near Pluto. They sound to me like bullies."

"What do you mean?"

"They demand that you do everything according to their conditions. They keep to themselves while they extract more and more information from you. They want total control. Classic signs of a bully, right there. He won't let you play in the playground unless he gets his way. I learned how to deal with bullies when I was six years old and Billy Burman and his gang tried to take my dead granddaddy's watch off my wrist. They said 'give us the watch or we'll crack these bottles over your head.'"

"And what did you do, Mr. Perkins?"

"I said 'No!'"

"And what did the gang do?"

"They cracked bottles over my head, punched me in the gut, and gave me a black eye."

"And the watch?"

"They left it."

"They left it? Why?"

"Because I dropped it on the ground and stomped on it." I shrugged my shoulders, "I didn't care if it worked. I only wanted it because it was my granddaddy's watch. I probably got a bigger beating than I would have, but the bullies didn't get their way."

"These are no schoolyard bullies. They are interstellar beings with capabilities we already know far surpass our own. Unfortunately, they hold all the cards, here, and I do mean *all*. Clearly, they know it. They have infiltrated our technology. They seem to know everything about us, but we know nothing about them. We are at their mercy. Getting a team to Pluto to find out what we can about them is going to be the biggest challenge mankind has ever undertaken. We've already made a 300 billion dollar bet on it. And we need you to join the crew."

I didn't even have to think about how to answer his request. "Administrator Hogarth, I appreciate that you didn't just scratch me off the list on account of my lack of, well, anything that would be of value to you. But, shoot. You've scared the bejeebers out of me with the helicopter and messages from aliens and 300 billion dollars and all that. I'd sooner jump in a pit of fanged snakes than go on your little excursion to Pluto."

He nodded, seeming relieved, "I understand."

"I wouldn't mind riding your fancy airplane back to North Carolina, though."

ΔvΔvΔvΔvΔ

The seven horticulture modules are shaped kind of like giant gas tanks. Inside, there is 514 square feet of space (almost thirty feet long and twenty-two feet across) where six wheels of planter racks are installed, leaving a small circle in the middle for the astronauts to pass through. It is filled with pink light that is in some way soothing but at the same time severe. There are little, green sprouts emerging from the planters now. One of the modules has a large work area free of plants. That is where we are standing—eh, floating.

"So, this is where all of you will spend most of your time," Sarah Foreman, the botanist, says. "Really, you're not astronauts at all. You are farmers. Remember, we expect you will be able to get eighty percent of your nutrition from the horticulture modules. But it's not just an expectation; it's a necessity. You will not have enough food with you, so if you don't tend your gardens, you *will* starve. Not only that, but carbon dioxide will build up. I'm sending you with the best that earth has to offer. These plants have the highest harvest index we can find. That means they have extremely high edible biomass ratios. You're getting dwarf tomatoes, dwarf peppers, radishes, herbs, dwarf white and sweet potatoes, and everybody's favorite: lettuce. I'm even sending you with dwarf plum trees. There's no excuse for you not to eat."

I say, "I just have one concern, Sarah."

"What's that, Jim?" she replies. The look on her face tells me she knows I'm probably going to say something silly.

"If we eat all these dwarf vegetables, is there any danger we'll come back, you know, as little people?"

"Always the jokester," she shakes her head. "No. In fact, you'll probably grow. When Commander Sykes stayed here for a year, he returned two inches taller."

"And I lost it two days later," says Commander Sykes.

"But you weren't feasting on dwarf carrots, were you Sykes?"

Next on the agenda is to receive our crew quarter assignments. We exit the horticulture area (which is in the mid-nadir section of the station) up through a tunnel into the Russian Node which is full of white, fabric storage bins and obstructed by conical hatches. The Russian modules, with the exception of the Service Module, are significantly narrower than the United States areas. Some of them are older, too, since they had been designed with MIR 2 in mind, but were repurposed for the ISS. You might think that, with all the newer components in place, the decision would have been made to do away with them because they are redundant, but it is their redundancy that caused the engineers to decide to keep them. If, for some reason, the U.S. segment or our crew quarters become uninhabitable, we will be able to evacuate to the Russian segment and seal ourselves in. Aside from Commander Filipchenko and Katia, there are two additional cosmonauts aboard: Valentin Gorbatko and Yury Marakov. They are making sure the Russian segment is ready for the long voyage, but they will not be joining us. They greet us warmly and give us a quick tour of the Russian Service Module. It was originally the core of the station providing central networking, avionics, mess hall, and crew quarters. I feel like I'm seeing history, because its age is very apparent, construction having been completed in 1986.

When we pass down the Russian node into one of the major additions to the station, Commander Tomlinson hands each of us a little bag, which contain our personal items we wanted to keep from home. From here, there are four entrances leading to four modules as spacious as the horticulture modules. One contains the crew quarters while another is a big centrifuge where we can take a shower, play games (including a golf simulator), and take a nap—all in one *g* gravity. One of them is pure stowage. The last contains the water processing facilities for the horticulture modules, air regeneration equipment, and the antimatter generator that will provide electric power for the station after the solar arrays have been fully retracted.

The crew quarters module has a public living area that, to NASA's credit, is very spacious, occupying one whole half of a 514 square-foot module, and has a homey look to it. Although they won't be of much use to us in zero-gravity, it is comforting nonetheless to see that there are sofas. Lamps have been fastened to the floor, and framed scenic vistas adorn the walls. On the right wall is a series of big windows. These provide the view I had been looking for in the cupola. A screen that must be at least seventy inches wide is fixed on the left wall, and I notice a BOSE sound system. The far wall is a big circle twenty-two feet wide with seven portals along the outer edge. The name of one of the crew members is above each portal. The center of the wall has an opening into a cylindrical space with a galley and dining table.

I float up to my portal and open it to find that my space is surprisingly spacious, though I'm not sure what I will do with all the room. The tall right wall and short left wall are both curved, following the module's circumference, while the ceiling and the floor are flat—likes spokes in a wheel. The front and back walls are also flat. There's a round window only a little bigger than my head on the right wall. A sleeping bag hangs on the back wall, upright, while the front wall has a mirror and a hygiene kit. A couple drawers are built into the left wall as well as a trash receptacle. Two laptops are anchored to the ceiling. It's stark, but at least the walls are a pleasant sky-blue color.

"Jim?" Tim's voice says from outside my portal. "Do you want to see them do the EVA or would you rather sleep?"

I float over to the portal and push it open. "I want to see the EVA, of course" I say.

∆v∆v∆v∆v∆

"I'm Deputy Miller with the Sedgwick County Sheriff's Office. Is this mister Jim Perkins?"

"Yes."

"Do you have a daughter named Betsy?"

"Yes."

"Betsy has been in a very serious accident involving a semi-truck. The radar-assisted cruise control malfunctioned on the highway. You need to come to St. Joseph's Hospital right away."

"I'm in Georgia," I said, stunned.

"It would be a good idea to get on the first flight you can straight here. The doctors say she, well, she probably won't survive the night. I'm sorry, Mr. Perkins. Is it true she has no spouse and no children?"

I couldn't speak. The woman on the other end of the line seemed to sense that, and just let me take a minute. I finally said, "No, no family. I'm the only family she has."

"I'm so sorry."

Six

Getting into an Extravehicular Activity space suit is quite an ordeal. I know personally because they made me do it to get experience floating around in that big pool at the Johnson Space Center—just in case. Now as I watch Kurt help Sanjin and Maria suit up, I feel a bit jealous. I bet a person can get quite a thrill from being out there free-floating above our planet. It almost seems that, since tomorrow they're going to send me three billion miles away, they should at least let me get a good look at the earth, first. But, life is full of little disappointments like this so I guess I'll just have to suck it up.

"I'm sorry you didn't have time for a camp-out," says Commander Sykes.

"We were breathing oxygen on the shuttle the whole time. But if we get the bends, it won't kill us," Maria says. With the suit's pants removed, she has crawled up inside with her head sticking out the top. Kurt is pulling the pajama bottoms (I call them that because the shoes are connected to the pants) up her legs. With the helmets fastened on, they go through all the pre-EVA checkouts they can before depressurization to make sure the suit is working properly. Everyone is in a good mood. I think that, as astronauts, this is exciting stuff for them. Nobody knows what the future holds. Nobody knows if they will ever get a chance to spacewalk again, or if this will be their last.

When the two astronauts are all dressed, Kurt clears out of the airlock and Commander Sykes helps him to close it, sealing them in. It takes a while for the airlock to depressurize. We can see the two astronauts in the chamber through a small window in the hatch. The way they are floating around in there, it reminds me of two big fish in a much-too-small aquarium.

The last two large solar arrays are fixed on a truss on the port side of the station. While Commander Tomlinson, Commander Sykes, and the team huddle around screens that show Sanjin and Maria's visor video feeds, I sneak back through the station to the cupola where I know I can get a good view of what's going on.

Through the windows, I see Sanjin in his puffy, white outfit as the Canadarm2 (one of the robotic arms) moves him slowly towards the solar arrays. The arrays are massive, 240 feet long, but they won't be of any use to us in deep space because we'll be so far from the sun. Not only that, but at the rate of speed we will be traveling, we really don't want to have big things sticking out that cover half the area of a football field. The smaller your profile, the less chance you have of getting hit by space debris.

As I watch, I find that I have to fight my eyes to keep my lids open. *I'm exhausted.*

Sanjin has reached the array. I push myself back up out of the cupola and out of Node 3 into Node 1. I try to get Commander Tomlinson's attention, but he is busy with the transfer of command from Commander Filipchenko. I get loud enough that Commander Tomlinson looks up, annoyed, to say, "What is it, Jim?"

"Do you need me for anything? I was thinking about going down for the night."

"No, we don't need you. Not at all." The way he says it makes it clear he means it. He doesn't want me on this mission. He wishes I wasn't here.

"Okay," I say. "Let me know if that changes. I'll be in my quarters." I slip down a tunnel, hang a right to the port side of the station and glide past the entrance of the centrifuge module on my way to the crew quarters.

Before I leave, though, I stop by Katia. "I'm turning in for the night."

"Night?" she grins. "It's night every ninety minutes, here."

Quietly, I say, "You know, Katia, you're young. You have your whole life ahead of you. You don't have to do this. I wish that you wouldn't. It's not too late to get out."

To my surprise, Commander Sykes, who was standing nearby, chimes in, "He's right. No one would criticize you."

She smiles and shrugs, "I am lucky to go. It's the chance of a lifetime."

The station is kept at seventy-two degrees Fahrenheit. I like it cooler than that for sleeping, so when I reach my cabin I kick off my pants and slip off my shirt. I realize that I'm still wearing the diaper I was so anxious not to soil. I shove it into the trash receptacle and throw off my shirt. Getting into my sleep pants and shirt in zero-g is a kind of a fun experience. Then I switch off the light and slink into the sleeping bag hanging on the wall. It's a strange sensation, just floating there. There's pressure on my back, and I can hardly tell that the sleeping bag is around me. They said astronauts have a tough time sleeping and usually only manage five or six hours a night. As tired as I am, I don't think I'll have that problem. I glance at my watch. It's 2:30 p.m. in the afternoon, Florida time. I guess I can be forgiven for being this tired since I was up all night prepping for the 4:27 a.m. launch.

My cabin is illuminated by the soft light of the earth coming in through the little round window. Tomorrow is the last time I will see earth this close. I hope I have a chance to get a good, long look at it before we launch out of orbit.

ΔvΔvΔvΔvΔ

By the time I made it to the hospital, my daughter was already dead.

She was the only family I had.

First, I grieved. Then, I got to thinking. A semi-truck's computer-operated radar assist cruise control happened to malfunction and kill my daughter right after I refused to go on the expedition to meet the aliens on Pluto. If these aliens were able to access enough information that they chose me and the other members of the crew by name, what limit was there to the access they had to the computers on earth? And if they had access, they probably also had control. Which made me think that my daughter's death was not an accident.

Crazy idea?

I don't know. But it made just enough sense to me that I gave a last-minute call to Administrator Hogarth and told him I'd changed my mind.

He said, "You're late to the party, Mr. Perkins. We have been training your replacement. It would be very difficult to slip you in so late."

"I know. But you said you wanted to do what they asked, and they asked for me. I am available."

"All right. I'll send the helicopter to pick you up."

If the aliens had killed my daughter, I wanted to meet them face to face. I wanted to tell the bullies "No."

And I wanted to beat their lights out and send them to hell, if that was possible.

ΔvΔvΔvΔvΔ

I wake up to a blaring alarm. I feel tremendous g-force on me like the worst roller coaster I've ever ridden. But I'm not being pulled back, I'm being pulled forward, with my chest pressed against the inside of my sleeping bag and my head hanging forwards. I lift my head and find I am facing the curved exterior wall that has the little window. Brilliant light floods in for only a second or two and then slowly dims to black. After about six seconds, the light returns. I'm a little dizzy.

The station is spinning fast, about ten times a minute. I might not be a rocket scientist, but I know that's not right.

My sleeping bag snaps free and I fall to slam onto the wall, my face against the window. The earth, close and filling my vision, disorientingly sweeps into view from one side and then out of view in the space of three seconds. Then, with a loud thud, something smashes into the outside of the window. As it drifts away, I realize that it is Sanjin in his tattered space suit. A shard of metal is sticking out of his shattered visor so I can't see his face, but I know it's him because the pants have red rings around them. (Maria's suit had no rings.) I have barely an instant to look at him before he's out of my line of sight. By the time he appears again, he is surprisingly distant. Pieces of debris are glistening in the sunlight against the blackness of space.

I look at my watch. It is 6:42 p.m..

The *g*-force is starting to get to me. It won't be long before I black out. I have to get out of here.

I struggle to pull myself along the wall towards the portal. Once I reach it, it's pretty tough to hoist myself up to it and labor through, but I manage it. On the other side, where there are the sofas, TV, and big windows, I can do nothing to stop myself from flopping from the portal onto the outer wall. The exit of the module is at the bottom of the room. Since I can't float there, I'll have to crawl along the wall to it. This makes me a little nervous because I'll have to cross the big windows. I'm not light. Raising my arm feels about six times harder than it would on earth, so I estimate I'm probably six times heavier now than I am on earth. That would be 1,170 pounds. I wonder if the window can withstand that much weight? Surely they wouldn't stick big windows like that on a space station heading to Pluto if they weren't virtually impenetrable. *Would they?*

Seven

Moving across the wall is intense work. I feel like I am crawling with an elephant on my back. In a way, I guess I am, but *I'm* the elephant, and I wasn't designed to carry this much weight. As I creep out onto the glass, my heart races. Pulling myself over the earth as it flies in and out of view every three seconds is not only terrifying, but also nausea-inducing. I'm getting really faint and dizzy. I have to reach the exit fast so I can move towards the center of the station and get away from this centrifugal force. The computer's female voice blares from speakers in the walls, "Automatic launch sequence initiated. Launch *T*-minus two minutes."

Launch sequence? What launch sequence? I think.

The glass doesn't creak or crack beneath me, as I feared it might. Even so, I'm relieved when I reach the other side. Fortunately, I don't have to try to climb the wall to get to the exit as it's right by the edge of the outer wall. I pass through it and, with my vision dimming, look up the tunnel. The blue handlebars will be difficult to use as I try to climb the tunnel because they were ideally placed for floating. I will be going in the starboard direction, but my body feels like I'm looking up.

"Launch *T*-minus one minute, thirty seconds."

I strain to pull myself up the first bar one hand over the other. I try to find places to brace my feet as I go: the rim of the entrance to the habitation module, a lip between two tunnel segments, and the mounting brackets of other bars.

I reach the centrifuge entrance. The centrifuge is the last place I want to be right now. I straddle the opening and pull myself across, feeling a bit more agile as I get closer to the center—now I feel like I'm only having to strain three times as hard as I normally would. All I have to do is go along one more tunnel segment to a node, then up a segment into the Russian section. Problem is, I'm blacking out. Darkness is closing in around me and my grip on the handlebars is weakening.

"*T*-minus one minute."

Ahead where the tunnel meets the node that leads up to the Russian section, someone suddenly drifts down head first. It's Katia. "Jimmy! Hurry, the computer initiated launch from earth orbit. We can't abort!"

"What?" I sleepily say.

She is floating down to me, but the farther she comes from the center of the station, the stronger the artificial gravity pulls her out towards me and she has to grab the bars and spin around so her legs fall down over her head. Once she is stable, she exclaims, "Someone started the automatic launch sequence. We're getting out of orbit. You have to be in your seat or you could die!"

This mission is getting off to a safe start, I think. *I've only been here a couple hours and already I'm in deadly peril.*

I try to pull myself towards her, but instead my hands slip and I slide down the vertical bar like a fireman down a pole. Knowing that I'll probably fall off the pole at the bottom and my body will squish at the end of the tunnel, I intertwine my fingers. My hands hit the bottom of the pole where a sharp-edged brace secures it to the wall. It feels like a 585-pound brick has crushed them.

She hurries down, shrieking, "Jimmy!" but the sudden weight throws her off and she ends up sliding down the pole on top of me. Now we're both hanging here. I can't hold on anymore and I lose my grip. I'm falling. I'm going to be squished at the far end of the tunnel.

But the opposite wall comes sailing towards me and I hit it with a big thump. My shirt rolls up and my skin squeaks loudly on the metal as I slide down the wall towards the tunnel termination. Katia, still dangling from the pole high above me, is being swung out with her feet in the middle of the tunnel. My slide slows to a stop before I reach it and, suddenly, I'm weightless.

"Good! The station is stabilized," Katia remarks with relief. "Hurry, come!"

I'm extremely dizzy now, but at least I don't feel faint. I swim in the air after her as we travel through the tunnel to the node, go up a segment to the Russian node, and hang a left towards the forwards section of the station. She is moving very fast and I clumsily struggle to keep up, banging against the walls and grabbing at anything to propel myself along. A claustrophobically narrow Russian storage module leads to a joining piece between the American and Russian areas. After that, we squeeze through a small portal and make it to Node 1.

The astronauts are all there, and in the American Science Lab beyond, struggling to put on their launch suits. It is chaos, with gloves and helmets floating around and everyone oriented differently. The computer's voice says, "Launch in *T*-minus thirty seconds."

Commander Sykes, from his position near the forward-most part of the Node, says firmly, "With all due respect, we don't have time for the suits. We should take launch positions now." He is staring directly at Commander Tomlinson, who is fumbling with his gear.

Commander Tomlinson says, "Suiting up is a prerequisite. You should know that. It's in the flight manual."

"I wrote some of that manual," Commander Sykes says under his breath. He exchanges a glance of frustration with Commander Filipchenko. Then he shouts, "Sarah and Kurt, you'll be joining me in the shuttle." To Commander Filipchenko, he says, "Viktor, if your guys want to come with us, we have space."

The cosmonauts follow Commander Sykes as he pulls himself forward into the American Science Lab.

"What are you doing?" Commander Tomlinson shouts. "You can't disconnect the shuttle! There isn't time!"

"I'm not disconnecting. You have thirteen people on this station, Commander Tomlinson, and launch restraints for only seven. Some of your crew will have to sit in the shuttle."

"That's not according to procedures. You could cause the station to be unbalanced."

"The shuttle isn't supposed to be connected during launch at all. It's already unbalanced. If not there, where do you want us to sit?"

Commander Tomlinson replies, "The cosmonauts should go to the Russian segment, and the shuttle crew should stay with me."

Commander Sykes says, "Everyone needs to be restrained. It will be very dangerous during launch."

"I said the Russians should go to the Service Module and your crew should join me. That's an order."

Everyone is just floating there, staring at the two commanders as they stare at each other, motionless.

The computer's voice says, "Launch in *T*-minus thirty seconds."

"You are putting the lives of your crew in danger," Commander Sykes says, low.

Commander Filipchenko puts a hand on Commander Sykes's shoulder, "It's okay. We'll go back." Then he and the two other cosmonauts shoot through the portal back into the Russian segment.

Commander Tomlinson's lips curl with a smile of victory. He says, "Everyone with me!" and leads the way forward through the American Science Lab to Node 2.

The seven spartan seats I had seen earlier line the circumference of the node. Commander Tomlinson calls, "Tim,

Shelby, Shiro, Nari, Katia, and Sarah, take a seat. The rest of you hold onto the handlebars and brace yourselves as well as you can."

Sarah hesitates, and protests, "But Jim was one of the original crew. Shouldn't he be in one of the seats?"

"Sarah," Commander Tomlinson says, "take a seat, I said."

The voice, "*T*-minus ten, nine, eight..."

Not looking at me, Sarah obliges and starts to fasten the restraints. A sign above the seat reads, "Jim Perkins."

"That seat is for Jimmy!" Katia exclaims.

"Katia, fasten your seatbelt!" Commander Tomlinson orders.

"I'll be fine," I say, gripping a handlebar. Commander Sykes and Kurt do their best to get ready for the impending launch. They are better situated than I am, with their feet buttressed on the rim of the entrance to the Science Lab, but I don't have time to make any adjustments because there is a deep rumble as the engines fire and the station starts to shudder.

The voice says, "One...and Launch of the International Space Station out of LEO for the planet Venus."

I heard somewhere that to get out of earth orbit, we will use almost as much fuel as the Saturn V rocket did when it launched from earth. Despite the considerable buttressing, questions still linger about how capable the station really is of surviving this catapult to 24,219 miles per hour.

Groans and creaks echo up from deep within the hull, and the vibration is intense. My feet swing aft and I tighten my grip on the bar. Just as the force of the launch really starts to pull me, I manage to press the tips of my toes on a piece of metal that's holding some wires together. That doesn't work too well, because my feet slip and I'm dangling from the bar by my hands. I feel kind of like I'm on a roller coaster that I really don't like and I'm just counting the seconds until it will stop. My hands are sweaty and my grip is loosening. Looking down, I am impressed with just how long the station is. It must be about 120 feet down to the place where I'll land if I fall: the back wall of Node 1. I get a foreboding sense of inevitability: I know that my fingers will slip and I will fall. I think Katia senses it too, because her face is really distraught as she looks at me from her seat across the node. There is nothing she or I can do.

Commander Sykes shouts, "Jim, hold on!"

But my hands come apart and I fall. On my way down, my feet hit the edge of the Science Lab and I tumble backwards. My head strikes the exercise machine and everything goes black.

Eight

Through blurred vision I see a Japanese flag. White all around with a big, red spot, the flag is waving slowly and strangely in an unearthly breeze. *We made it to Pluto, and Shiro planted a Japanese flag,* I think.

No, my vision is clearing, and I see the walls of the lab, tangled with wire and equipment. The red spot, undulating in and out like a giant amoeba, is growing. I am drifting backwards towards the center of the module from the corner where I was lodged, and the blob is following me. My head is throbbing, and I feel a strange tingling sensation in my left arm. Halfway down my forearm is a bend where it must be broken. Blood is shooting out of my other arm in bubbles and streams that quickly join to the blob. It is a rather surreal thing to see, one's blood flowing out and creating a floating blob that's as big as your head and looks almost alive. In my delirious state, I kind of want to poke it and see what happens.

But suddenly I feel intense, searing pain and it jolts me fully awake like a lightning bolt.

"Jim!" I hear Shelby's voice behind me. She maneuvers me around and when she sees the trauma to my arm, concern creases her face, "You're pretty badly hurt." She moves quickly to stop the bleeding from the gash in my left arm by pressing a towel on it. "C'mon, we need to get you to the European Lab." She pulls me past Commander Tomlinson, who just stares at my injury, kind of shell-shocked.

Commander Sykes scowls at Commander Tomlinson and says, "I'm going to check on Viktor and the guys." He sails back through the American Lab into Node 1.

Shelby, Katia, Tim, Nari, Shiro, and Kurt maneuver me carefully through Node 1 and to the left into the European Science Module. There, Shelby flips down an operating table and straps me onto it. She says, "I need to stitch you up and set the bones. I'm going to give you some anesthesia."

"Okay," I faintly say.

"I'm probably going to need to use metal plates and drill holes in your bones. Is that all right?"

"Whatever you say, doc. Just make the pain go away."

She smiles, "You're okay." She places a mask over my mouth and nose and tells Tim to hold it, which he does. She fastens a glass vial to a nozzle and twists some knobs on the panel above where I am lying. I hear a hissing sound. "Katia, look in that drawer for a pouch with a *TraumaDex* label." It doesn't take long for me to start to black out.

ΔvΔvΔvΔvΔ

I wake up to a searing pain. I am still strapped to the table, but my arm is in a cast and a sling holds it in place above my chest. It is dark in the European module, but there is light in Node 2 and I hear Shelby saying, "It will probably take his bones twice as long to heal in space. The transcranial Doppler came out okay, but that doesn't mean he's out of the woods. He could be hemorrhaging and I just can't see it."

"At least the Russians are okay," Commander Sykes says. "They were smart enough to sit in the Soyuz."

My head starts to throb with a headache. I close my eyes.

Commander Tomlinson says, "Listen, the station was designed to support seven people and now we have thirteen. What are we supposed to do about that? Even if we eat like mice, there won't be enough food. We won't have enough water, we'll have too much waste, the oxygen will run out, carbon dioxide will pile up, we'll expend our carbon filters, there will be problems we haven't even thought of yet. Can you take the extra crew on the shuttle and jettison back to earth?"

Commander Sykes replies, "We're already 120,000 kilometers from earth and we'd have to overcome 40,000 kilometers per hour of velocity the wrong direction. It's not an option."

Commander Tomlinson asks, "What about Soyuz?"

"Same difference. And that would only get you three people, even if it had the fuel."

Commander Tomlinson: "You sound like you don't want to try to solve this problem."

"Trust me, I want to get back home."

"So, what do we do to get you there?"

"We pull an Oberth maneuver at Venus that points us back towards earth and we abort the mission."

There is silence for a moment. Commander Tomlinson says, "Abort the mission? Are you freaking insane? We can't do that."

"Why not?" Commander Sykes says. "At this point, the mission is a failure. Like you said, we will run out of food and oxygen. We'll show up to Pluto with several corpses. That's not acceptable."

"It should be acceptable to you. I didn't hear you calling for an abort of this program when Discovery was lost."

"Everyone who flew on the shuttles knew the risks, including me."

"As dangerous as they were, you could say that everyone who flew on the shuttles was delusional, including you," Commander Tomlinson murmurs. "Listen, they're expecting us on Pluto on November the 30th, 2021, and if we're not there, we won't have another chance to meet them."

"I don't buy that. If they want to meet us, they'll wait. It would be a delay of 150 days, max. When the station reaches earth, it can resume LEO and NASA can resupply it. We just have to consider this a trial. A successful trial."

Commander Tomlinson states, "We can't abort the mission. Not on my watch."

"This isn't your call. We need to ask Houston."

"As you know, talking to Houston is a bit of a problem right now."

"We have forty-nine days between now and our Venus encounter. That should be enough time to fix our communications."

Shelby's voice says, "Jim, can you hear me?"

I open my eyes to see her standing over me in the darkness. I smile, "I'm awake. Arm hurts, head hurts, but I'm awake."

"I'll give you some more Percocet."

"Will that make me sleep?"

"It might make you sleepy, but it won't necessarily put you out."

While she's fiddling with the IV, I ask, "What happened? Why did we launch early?"

"When the Origins capsule was separating from the station, one of its thrusters wouldn't stop firing. It sent the station on a spin. After it separated from the station, there was an explosion. Origins hit Sanjin and Maria and snapped their tethers."

Commander Tomlinson saunters in with his hands in his pockets and says, "I guess you're not going to be able to do your chores. I'll have Katia pick up your slack."

"I still have my right arm. I can do the chores."

Commander Tomlinson asks Shelby, "When can he get off this cot?"

"I don't want him doing much of anything except the BDM." The BDM (Bone Density Maintainer) is a vibration machine we get to stand on for twenty minutes every day. Some researchers found out that vibration does wonders for keeping astronauts' bones strong in microgravity. It's even better than exercise.

"Jimmy!" Katia says as she floats into the module. "How are you feeling?"

"I think I'm ready for my first round of space golf."

Katia asks Shelby, "Can he come with me? I want him to see something."

Shelby replies, "That's okay. But no space golf."

ΔvΔvΔvΔvΔ

Katia and I are looking out a window at the earth. I am astounded by how far we have come and how small our home already looks. It's about the same size as a ping pong ball held at arm's length. I can make out Australia on the lower left side of the globe, with China, Japan, and the rest of east Asia rimming the edge.

Katia remarks, "We are half the distance of the moon to the earth. Really puts things in perspective, doesn't it?"

"Yes," I say, "space is pretty darn big." That's another of my comments that would go nicely on a plaque with Armstrong's "One small step for a man..."

"This is your last chance to see it this close before we go to Pluto," Katia says.

"Last chance? Sykes says we'll probably turn around at Venus and go back."

Katia raises her eyebrows, "Why? Commander Tomlinson told me everyone is onboard."

"Commander Sykes isn't."

ΔvΔvΔvΔ

We are all in Node 2 because Commander Tomlinson has called a meeting. He says, "I know things are much different than we planned and trained for. Our biggest hurdle at this point is that we can't reach NASA. I have spoken with each of you and I know most of you want to proceed with the mission. Anyone here who thinks we should abort at Venus, raise your hand."

Commander Filipchenko immediately raises his hand. Valentin and Yury quickly follow. Filipchenko says, "I cannot go to Pluto. I've been in space six months already, and now my mother has cancer."

Commander Sykes says, "I want to get a directive from Houston. If we can't get the antenna array back up, we must abort the mission."

Commander Tomlinson says, "To do that, we need to fix the communications array. That means an EVA. The station's EMUs are gone, so if your team could get the suits from the shuttle, that would be great, Eric. The obvious person to do the EVA is Tim since he is our tech guy. I also nominate Filipchenko because he has done more EVA's than anyone here. Does that sound like a plan?"

Commander Sykes says, "Sounds good to me."

Everyone nods in agreement.

"Good. It's now almost 2200 hours. With the exception of Jim, who took a senior siesta earlier today, the rest of us have been awake for at least forty hours. How about we call it a day and start things up again in the morning at 0700? Filipchenko and Tim, you'll need to freshen up, eat, and get on the bike with your oxygen as soon as possible in the morning. Sarah can lead the rest of us in our horticulture activities so we can start getting in the swing of things right away. Those plants are our lifeblood. Does anyone have anything else?"

"Shouldn't we do a campout?"

"You mean sleep in the airlock? Normally I'd say 'yes,' but in this case, I want you to have as much sleep as possible, given the circumstances. You'll sleep in your quarters, tonight."

"Where should Viktor's and my crews sleep?" asks Commander Sykes.

Commander Tomlinson replies, "How many can sleep in the Russian Service Module?"

"Two."

"Okay, two of the Russians can sleep in there. Everyone else will need to share quarters in the Crew Quarters Module, for now."

Everyone seems eager to get to bed and, without much else said, drifts back towards the crew quarters.

I, on the other hand, don't feel much like going to my quarters. Having taken advantage of a "senior siesta" (as Tomlinson so eloquently called it), and also having slept for three hours during and after surgery, you wouldn't say I have a major sleep deficit. On top of that, the last time I was in my quarters, Sanjin's corpse was floating outside the window, so I don't have very homey feelings for the place. Commander Tomlinson extinguishes the lights so that only dim, blinking, green equipment lights illuminate the passages.

I do, however, want to catch another glimpse outside the big windows in the lounge, so I follow everybody else through the American Science Lab, Node 1, the Russian Storage Module, and into the cramped Russian node with cone-shaped hatches obstructing easy passage. From there, it's down and to port where the crew quarter module is at the end of the tunnel.

In the crew quarters module, I wish everyone goodnight as they enter their own portals. Then I focus my attention outside the windows, where the starry view is spectacular, with the Milky Way diagonally crossing the upper right in resplendent glory like I've never seen it before, not even way out in the remotest nighttime fields of Kansas wheat. I also see three very bright stars dotting the center of the view. The one on the left is very clearly orange. The other two, close together, are also orange, but not nearly as colorful. I'm pretty sure the one on the left is Mars. As bright as they are, the other two must be Jupiter and Saturn. It is almost unthinkable to believe that, if Houston orders us to continue the mission, we will be passing by both of those giant planets.

Suddenly, a noise from one of the portals catches my attention. Commander Tomlinson is emerging. He spots me and immediately floats down. As if we are the best of buds, he says, "Quite a view, Jim, isn't it?"

"Yes," I agree. "It is."

"Makes you hope the mission doesn't end," he muses. "See those two bright lights to the right? That is Jupiter and Saturn."

"Hey, bingo! That's what I thought. Guess I might make a decent astronaut, after all."

He grins. "We will be the first people to see them with our own eyes. Saturn has always been my favorite planet. I can't imagine what it will be like to see it in person. We're the luckiest people on earth, to be on this mission."

I point out, "But we're not on earth, anymore."

"No, we're not." He clears his throat, "Listen, I want you to know I have a newfound respect for you. Two broken bones and you didn't even flinch. You're a pretty tough old-timer, aren't you?"

I shrug, "A man's bones don't make him tough. It's what he does when the going gets tough that shows how tough he is."

"I like that." He gives my back a slap, "Make sure you rest up. If I were you, I'd be wanting to head home."

"Head home? Why?"

"Shelby says it could take you nine to twelve months to heal."

"Nine to twelve months?" I say, stunned. I think she said six months.

"Yes," he asserts. "She says bones take twice as long to heal in space. And, with your age...it just won't be an easy process." He places a hand on my shoulder, "But don't worry. We've got your back. We will pick up your slack."

"I'll manage," I say.

He nods, "I appreciate your enthusiasm. Now get some sleep, old-timer. It should be easy because you don't even have a roommate. Yury was snoring like a rocket, that's why I'm out here. You have a good night."

"You too," I say.

He drifts away into the tunnel. Before he proceeds, he glances back at me, his eyes glowing fluorescent green in the dim light, and then pulls himself out of view.

Nine

While Tim and Filipchenko are breathing pure oxygen in preparation for their EVA, the rest of us are getting acquainted with our horticulture modules. I always wanted to do some cultivating, but I was away from home too much to devote my time to the TLC that plants need. Now, gardening will be my chief activity.

Sarah is excited to show us that some of the seedlings she brought have already sprouted. It's the beans, of course. Even though we've been away from earth for merely a day, it's nice to see something green sticking out of the soil. You might think we would be doing hydroponics, but water has a tendency to seep in all directions in microgravity, so that really isn't an option. Instead, we have compost, and it stinks. This is kept in buckets that fortunately have lids. We have a supply of worms that are supposed to breed and last us the entire journey, but if they happen to die, we also have a stash of frozen worms that we can reanimate. I suppose I should take pride in the fact that, as the station maid, one of my chief duties will be to supply everyone's compost barrels with nourishment from the station's toilets. There's no more important work than playing a pivotal part of the food chain. If a man can't feel pride in his work, why work? Here, I'm highly motivated.

Those of us who were selected to go on the mission to Pluto have already had a lot of farmer practice in training. But now, we have six crew members who need to be brought up to speed. One of them is preparing for his EVA, but the other five listen attentively to Sarah as she shows us around.

She explains that the horticulture modules, despite their reliance upon the age-old techniques of composting, planting, and watering, are technologically advanced, as are the plants themselves. The plants are part of what Sarah calls a "Transgenic Arabidopsis Gene Expression System." She points to a monitor where a series of trailing, white lines appear in green boxes, each with a label. The labels read:

```
SOL-LYC-A0101
SOL-LYC-A0102
LAC-SAT-A0101
LAC-SAT-A0102
SOL-TUB-A0101
SOL-TUB-A0102
PHA-VUL-A0101
PHA-VUL-A0102
```

"The labels refer to the name of the plant, its berth location, and its vector coordinates within the berth. So 'SOL-LYC' is *Solanum lycopersicum*, 'LAC-SAT' is *Lactuca sativa*, SOL-TUB is *Solanum tuberosum*, and 'PHA-VUL' is *Phaseolus vulgaris* and they are located in berth A. What you see on the screen is each plant's roots. We added a protein called GFP to their genes. Cameras with fluorescent lights will make the roots glow so you can monitor them on the computers. A plant that is underperforming can be quickly replaced to save precious growth space from waste."

She shows us two buckets that are strapped in a corner. "When you harvest, these things won't just pop into cans and be ready to eat. You'll need to get the beans out of their pods, discard a lot of stems and inedible debris, and do some cleanup. You can use these buckets for that work, and of course everything you discard will go straight to the compost."

I say, "I just have one question."

She crosses her arms in front of her chest, "What's that, Jim?"

"What the heck is growing in there?"

She smiles, "You'll need to learn the Latin names quickly if you want to eat."

By now, the two spacewalkers are ready for the excursion outside to take a look at one of the dish antennas, so we all go up to Node 1 to help with pre-EVA activities. While everyone else is busy, Commander Tomlinson takes me aside to ask if I'm feeling up to starting my cleaning duties because he says today he needs Katia to man the robotic arm controls.

This puts me in a bit of a pickle. I know commander Shelby doesn't want me to do any work, just yet. She wants me on that confounded BDM machine. Now, I'm not an astronaut and I don't know much about how to operate the station, but I do know I certainly didn't come into space just to sit on a big vibrator for hours on end. So, I tell Commander Tomlinson I'm ready to get to work.

He hands me a thick binder labeled *International Space Station Housekeeping and Sanitation Group (HSG) In-Flight Housekeeping Manual.* He says, "Make sure you follow these procedures. And, Jim, I'll be checking."

"Yes, sir."

As soon as he leaves, the first thing I decide to do is check out the space vacuum cleaner. I set the book adrift while I work on freeing it from its place in the ceiling. From the interior speakers all over the station, I hear the radio chatter as the spacewalk begins. I'd kind of like to watch this one, too, now that I'm better rested, but duty calls.

To my disappointment, the vacuum cleaner is not much different from any terrestrial vacuum, the major difference being that, in space, it doesn't weigh anything, no matter how much dirt it gobbles up. Very simply designed, it is just a cylinder with a hose sticking out one end, and in its carrying case is an assortment of pipes and nozzles to affix to the hose. I take the vacuum to Node 3, where the exercise equipment, the toilet, the cupola, and most of the cleaning supplies are.

There, after I attach the pipes and nozzle to the vacuum's hose, I set about trying to assemble a little cleaning dolly that I can take with me as I sanitize each module. After about five minutes, the accordion door to the outhouse opens and Commander Sykes emerges. I'm startled because I didn't know anyone was in there. He is looking grim-faced and his eyes are red. I wonder if he has been crying. I guess, since he lost two members of his crew yesterday, that wouldn't be a surprise. We've kind of just gone about our business as if that never happened.

In an unusually cheerful voice he asks, "How's your arm, Jim?"

"If I move it, I get a sharp pain, but as long as I keep it still, it's bearable. How are you?"

He looks to the side, kind of like he wants to make sure nobody is listening. "I hope we do the right thing, here."

"What is the right thing?"

"If we can't make contact with earth, what's the point of making first contact? We need to talk with Houston. If we can't, we should abort the mission."

I nod, "That makes sense. I guess it's very important we get the antenna array fixed, then."

"Yes," he says. "It's critical." He motions to the vacuum cleaner and says, "You know what we call that?"

"A vacuum cleaner?"

He smiles, "It's the only piece of equipment that doesn't suck on the International Space Station."

We exchange a chuckle, and he quickly evacuates the module.

In my truck, I did a routine wipe-down once a week, so in addition to vacuuming up here, I think it would be a good idea to wipe every surface that anyone touches. Once I have strapped together an arrangement of supplies to a box that I think will be serviceable, I realize I have forgotten all about the housekeeping manual. *Heaven forbid Commander Tomlinson catch me without it.* It should have been the first thing I stuffed in my makeshift dolly. I float back to the European Lab where I left it and find it has sailed its way to the very back of the module where the ultrasound machine is.

I snatch it and am surprised by how big it really is. It must be a thousand pages long, or close to it. I go back to Node 3 and sneak down into the cupola to start my compulsory reading and see if I can catch a glimpse of earth.

Outside, the earth is the size of a grape held at arm's length. Small and slight against the vast backdrop of the starry universe, it is, as they say, like a blue marble. I'm a little unsettled that I can't distinguish anything on its surface except blue and white. This brings home the reality of how far from home I am. The moon, two times closer, is to the left, and also about the size of a marble. But, to my wonderment, it doesn't look like the moon I am used to seeing. Its terrain is unfamiliar and more uniformly bright and bare. I realize that I'm looking at the far side of the moon, something only a handful of humans have ever had the chance to do. Despite not being an astronaut or ever wanting to go to space, I can't help but feel a sense of awe.

I can also see Tim and Filipchenko perched by their feet on the end of one of the robotic arms as it lofts them towards the dish antenna. I know Katia is at the robotic arm's controls, and I have to admire her competence. When I saw them practicing maneuvering the robotic arms, it seemed very complicated to me, unnecessarily so, but what do I know? I'm used to pushing two pedals and spinning a wheel.

I open the manual. The front page says:

International Space Station Housekeeping and Sanitation Group (HSG) In-Flight Housekeeping Manual
Mission Operations Directorate
Systems Division
March 20TH, 2020
National Aeronautics and Space Administration
Lyndon B. Johnson Space Center
Houston, Texas

I flip to page two:

United States
Systems Operations Data File JSC-48513-E1
INTERNATIONAL SPACE STATION
HOUSEKEEPING & SANITATION GROUP (HSG)
IN-FLIGHT MAINTENANCE MANUAL
EXPEDITION 130 FLIGHTS
MARCH 20TH, 2020
APPROVED BY:
Jordan Smart
Book Manager
Susan S. Orwell
Lead, DF53/Mechanisms & Maintenance Group
Gordon M. Thompson
SODF Coordinator
ACCEPTED BY:
Mitchell T. Swank
SODF Manager
This document is under the configuration control of the Systems Operations Data
File Control Board (SODFCB).

I can tell this is going to be fun reading, already. Page three:

```
United States
Systems Operations Data File JSC-48513-E1
20 MAR 2020 ISS IFM ii
Incorporates the following:
CR: IFM U10
IFM U12
IFM U16
IFM U20
MF U137
MF U152
MF U175
```

I start to skip pages for the table of contents which, as it turns out, is five pages long. The last item is:

```
E.35  MOD  TEMPERATURE  CCAA  RACK  CLEANING  (LAB1S6)
........... 753
```

This manual is 753 pages long. I guess even the housekeeper on the international space station needs to be a genius.

As I peruse the items listed in the contents, I think most of this must be a bunch of unnecessary mumbo-jumbo explaining things that any nincompoop wouldn't need a manual to do, but then something catches my eye that leads me to believe I am mistaken.

```
3.1.302 LAB BACTERIA/CHARCOAL FILTER INSPECT, CLEAN, AND R&R
```

Inspecting and cleaning a bacteria filter sounds pretty important. I flip to the page listed for that procedure:

3.1.302 LAB BACTERIA/CHARCOAL FILTER INSPECT, CLEAN, AND R&R

(ISS IFM/5A - ALL/FIN A) Page 1 of 5 pages
08 MAR 2020
2785.doc
START_IMS
OBJECTIVE:
Remove and replace expended Bacteria or Charcoal Filters (three each
standoff) one standoff at a time or replace Charcoal Filter with Bacteria
Filter.
LOCATION:
Installed: Lab Standoffs LAB1SD1,3,5 and LAB1PD1,3,5
Stowed: √Maintenance and Assembly Task Supplement (MATS)
DURATION:
45 minutes
PARTS:
Bacteria Filters (four) (P/N SV810010-1) or
Charcoal Filters (four) (P/N SV821776)
MATERIALS:
Gray Tape
TOOLS REQUIRED:
ISS Common IVA Tool Kit:
Kit E:
Ratchet, 1/4" Drive
6" Ext, 1/4" Drive
Kit F:
5/16" Socket, 1/4" Drive

Kit H:
Scissors
Kit J:
Connector Pliers
REFERENCED PROCEDURE(S):
1.402 SMOKE DETECTOR DEACTIVATION
1.401 SMOKE DETECTOR ACTIVATION
2.503 CCAA FAN SPEED DECREASE
SAFING
CAUTION
To maintain air circulation in the Lab, execute
this procedure one standoff at a time.
CAUTION
Fan speed must be decreased before closing
Cabin Air Damper Assembly.
  1. For operating CCAA (LAB1S6 or LAB1P6), perform {2.503 CCAA FAN
    SPEED DECREASE} (SODF: ECLSS: NOMINAL: THC) to 4000 rpm.
  3.1.302 LAB BACTERIA/CHARCOAL FILTER INSPECT, CLEAN, AND R&R

Just as I'm thinking it would be a lot more helpful to have someone teach me how to do this than try to learn it from this unintelligible manual, I am startled by a loud bang right by my head. The robotic arm has collided with the cupola.

Ten

The arm, with Tim and Commander Filipchenko perched on the end, swings away from the cupola in a wide arc and, with a force that sends tremors through the whole station, slams into the antenna array. Commander Filipchenko is flung out over the array. He is rapidly tumbling end over end from the station. For a moment, he is nearly invisible in the shadow of the station, but then appears brilliantly white in the light of the sun. Meanwhile, the robotic arm oscillates in place, striking the antenna array over and over again while Tim struggles to avoid being crushed. His desperate voice can be heard over the radio shouting, "STOP THE ARM! STOP THE ARM!" Debris from the array is scattering everywhere.

Commander Filipchenko, calmer and in some way distant, is saying, "Station, my tether is free and I am drifting. Do you read me?" He is now already a football field away.

Commander Sykes' voice is on the radio, "Viktor, use your SAFER. Use the attitude control."

But Viktor's voice, now obscured by static and increasingly rattled, is shouting, "Sta—, I—loose! My SAFER—not funct— Station! Katia! I—help!" He is flying in nearly the opposite trajectory that the station is heading, and is now merely a white dot in the distance.

Katia's voice shrieks, "Viktor, use the SAFER! Viktor!"

The robotic arm has ceased movement and Tim is left floating beside it by his tether. He is still.

Nari's voice cries, "Tim!"

He slowly raises himself up, saying, "I'm okay. Where's Viktor?"

Commander Filipchenko is now barely visible in the distance. Tim spots him and calls out, "Viktor! Viktooor!" He untethers himself and pulls out the controller for his SAFER. "I'm going after him!" he says. Thrusters on the SAFER fire, and he begins to drift away from the station towards the aft.

"Tim, listen," Commander Sykes' voice is on the radio.

"What's the range on this?"

Commander Sykes: "Tim, the SAFER does not have the fuel to make it."

Tim is still accelerating away from the station.

Commander Tomlinson shouts, "Tim, turn around now. That's an order! You can't match the velocity or the distance."

The speck of light that is Commander Filipchenko falls beyond my field of vision.

"Tim!" cries Nari. "Come back! You can't make it! Tim!"

Tim is now past the aft section of the station where the giant external fuel tanks are.

Tim says, "Nari. I'm coming back. I can't reach him." He slowly turns around and begins to return to the station.

ΔvΔvΔvΔvΔ

Commander Tomlinson winds the hatch's crank handle counter clockwise and locks it into place. Nari impatiently helps to lift the hatch up vertically along grooves in the side walls until the airlock is fully exposed. Then, crying, she rushes in to hug and kiss Tim, still in his space suit and helmet.

It takes nearly an hour to get his tools, SAFER, and suit off and stowed away. When that is complete, Valentin starts to badger Katia in Russian. He becomes increasingly agitated.

Commander Tomlinson says, "Valentin! Enough! It wasn't her fault! It was a malfunction! Let's just try to find out what went wrong."

We all huddle around to examine Commander Filipchenko's waist tether. The metal, hooked clip has no sign of stress. No matter how hard Commander Tomlinson tries, he is unable to make the latch loosen.

"The problem must have been with the suit, then," comments Shiro. He has been so quiet during the mission so far that I almost forgot he was with us.

"It looks that way, yes," says Commander Tomlinson.

Shiro says, "I thought I heard him say his SAFER wasn't functioning."

"Yes, he did say that," Tim agrees. "And he certainly wasn't able to use it."

Commander Tomlinson looks at Kurt, "You did the SAFER checkout. Did you notice any problem?"

"No, I didn't."

"Did you follow procedure?"

"Yes, I think I did."

"You followed all the procedures, Kurt?" Commander Tomlinson questions.

"Yeah, absolutely."

Commander Tomlinson says, "Bring me the Cue Card. Maybe something was logged before, on the last EVA."

Kurt retrieves the card and, looking sheepish, hands it to Commander Tomlinson.

Commander Tomlinson examines the card and says, "Kurt, what is this? You didn't record anything on this card. You're supposed to record the N2, power, and battery from the display, after the test."

"The levels were all over spec. I was in a rush, so I thought I would jot it down later."

"But you should have written them down when you did the checkout."

Kurt holds a breath, then exhales. "Yes," he admits. "I should have."

"This is why it's so important to follow procedure. Most of everything an astronaut, or even all of NASA does, is for safety. Let this be a lesson for all of us: follow procedure. Kurt, do you agree?"

"I agree, I should have followed procedure. But I do know the levels were correct. That wasn't the problem."

"If you had written them down, we could verify that," asserts Commander Tomlinson. "Now, we'll never know."

"But I do know. I *saw* them! The nitrogen was 91%. The power was 69%. The battery was 70%. That's well above spec."

"The fact is the unit didn't function when Viktor needed it, and now he's gone. Humans are error-prone. We all are. You might have misread something. Or, you might have made some other mistake. To perform the checkout, you have to turn it on, flip the right switch, and wait while it fires the thrusters twenty-four times. You're not supposed to leave it on for more than sixty seconds. What if you didn't turn it back off? What if you flipped the wrong switch? Possibilities for human error are endless. Procedures minimize error. Follow procedure, Kurt."

"Writing numbers in the log would not have saved Viktor."

"You lied to us, Kurt. You said you followed every procedure, but we see that you didn't. I have no confidence that you did anything you say you did because there's no evidence. These things have been hashed out by millions of hours of study and practice by people and computers that are much smarter than we are. Do you think you're smarter than a whole team of analysts and computers, Kurt? Is *one man* smarter than all of NASA's best process managers and scientists, not to mention the Lockheed Martin engineers?"

"No," Kurt shakes his head.

"I think we're on the same page, then," Commander Tomlinson says. Then, to my surprise, without skipping a beat he looks straight at me and says, "On that note, have you finished reading the *Housekeeping and Sanitation Manual*, Jim?"

"Not yet."

"Then you have work to do, and it certainly isn't here eavesdropping." He smiles, "Nobody keeps a maid who's a gossip."

Eleven

I retreat to the cupola where I can watch the earth getting tinier and tinier as I read the manual from cover to cover. By the time I'm done, the earth is smaller than a pea held at arm's length and the moon is a bright dot the size of a grain of rice. We have come so far in one day. And yet we are forty-eight days from reaching Venus and 106 days from the sun, assuming we continue the mission and get a speed boost from Venus. We are tiny, little buggers, and the universe is a big son of a gun.

Put that one down in the famous sayings to give Armstrong a run for his money.

The manual leaves me little more equipped to clean and sanitize the station than I was before I read it. So, I think I'll ask the person who lived here for a year already and probably did a lot of cleaning and sanitizing in that time, Commander Sykes.

I wander around the station for a few minutes on the prowl for him until I hear his and Commander Tomlinson's subdued voices coming from the Japanese lab. They sound like they're having an argument, but they don't want anybody to hear them.

Commander Tomlinson says, "But he isn't worthy of that trust."

Calmly, Commander Sykes says, "I've been on five missions with him. I trust him because he's proven he's worthy of that trust."

"He lied to us, to all of us. A bald-faced lie without even a twinge of guilt. I think that speaks to a different kind of personality, don't you? Someone who can lie so easily like that... It's scary."

"He made a mistake, and I think that had you not been berating him so publicly, he probably wouldn't have."

"Oh, so his lie is my fault? You're very talented at scrambling up the truth, Eric."

"I didn't say that what he did was your fault. I said he probably wouldn't have lied if the conversation had been held in private using different language."

"But what about the SAFER? It wasn't functional, yet he claims that he tested it."

"The checkout doesn't prove anything. The computer is programmed to fire twenty-four bursts of nitrogen, and then the readout gives the percentages. That doesn't mean the unit was 100% functional."

"The Lockheed Martin engineers created and programmed that test. Are you saying they would create something bogus that doesn't actually do anything to keep us safe?"

"No, I'm saying that a checkout with no fault is not a fail-safe against a problem."

"Well I'm saying that we don't know if he even completed the checkout, and given the fact he lied about the Cue Card, chances are he lied about the whole thing, too. A person who tells a single lie is a liar and cannot be trusted. I think you're showing a serious lack of discernment, here. Kurt cannot be relied upon to follow procedures, and he cannot be trusted to tell the truth. He needs to be monitored closely. We need to put a SPHERES on him."

"No. I won't do that, and you shouldn't either."

"Fine, but when he screws up next time, I won't ask for your opinion. I'll do what needs to be done."

Commander Tomlinson suddenly floats into Node 2 from the Japanese Module and spots me. He smiles, "Hello, old-timer. Eavesdropping, again?"

"I had a question for Commander Sykes."

"What's the question?"

"I wanted him to show me how to do a thing or two from the cleaning manual."

Commander Tomlinson nods, "And you're asking him instead of me because he has more experience on the station."

"Yes," I confirm.

"Sounds logical. But nobody knows procedures better than I do."

"I can't disagree with that," I say. And I mean it, though I don't intend it to be a compliment. He has made it blatantly obvious that no one knows, values, or knocks people upside their heads with procedures better than he does.

"Go ahead and ask him. But after this, please get some sleep."

"It's only nine o'clock."

"Yes, and we need to transition to the standard flight plan."

"Standard flight plan?"

"Yes, according to NASA's schedule, we should be up at 6 o'clock."

"That's great by me. But, who's to say what time six o'clock is, out here?"

"We're moving to GMT. It's protocol. We need to follow protocol. That means right now it's actually one o'clock in the morning. I'd get to bed as soon as possible, if I were you, because in five hours we'll need to be up."

"Wow. Time moves fast in space," I facetiously comment.

He goes on his way, and I enter the Japanese module to find Commander Sykes floating there with his arms tightly folded across his chest in his usual way. He looks like he's deep in thought.

I say, "Commander Sykes?"

He looks up, "Hello, Jim. What's up?"

"I read this manual, but I wondered if you might be able to show me how to do some of the stuff in here. It's a little over my head, I'm afraid."

"Sure, no problem. We can get started tomorrow. Tomlinson wants us to move to GMT time so we need to get to bed ASAP."

"Yes, he told me. Apparently, we're going to lose three hours of sleep."

"Yes, we are. And I have to do a spacewalk, tomorrow."

"You? For what?"

"The antenna array is shot to pieces. I'm going to go out there to see what I can do."

I frown, "But aren't you a little worried? I mean we've lost three people on spacewalks. It doesn't seem safe."

"Yes, I am worried. That's why I'm doing it myself."

"Be careful. We need you."

He smiles, "You don't have to worry about me. I'll be just fine."

We float back to the crew quarters module together. By the time we reach it, Commander Tomlinson has ordered the computer to shut off all the interior lights, and we are bathed in surreal, flickering green light from the equipment. Saying a quick goodnight to Commander Sykes, I enter my portal. I've only been there a minute or two, taking a quick peek out the window and opening up my sleeping bag before there is a faint knock on my door. I open it to see Katia there, holding a tablet in her hand.

"May I come in?" she whispers.

I nod, and open the portal hatch wider for her to pass through. Once she's inside, she closes the hatch herself and faces me. "There's something wrong, Jimmy."

"What is it?"

"Viktor should not have died."

"How do you mean?"

She shows me the screen:

$P(A \cap B \cap C) = 1.45e{-}38$

I look at her blankly. She has a PhD in mathematics. I don't.

She explains, "We experienced three failures during the same EVA that caused Viktor's death. First, the robotic arm went haywire. Then, his tether broke free. Finally, his SAFER failed to operate. The statistical probability of all those failures happening at the same time is one chance in 145 undecillion."

"Undecillion?"

"Yes, this number," she taps on her screen.

145,000,000,000,000,000,000,000,000,000,000,000,000

"Wow," I say. "That's a big number."

"Yes. It is *many* more stars than are in the whole universe. This should not have happened. Viktor should not be dead. This means it couldn't have been my fault. I didn't kill him." She starts to cry.

"Of course you didn't kill him," I encourage. "It was an accident."

She wipes her eyes, "It was no accident. The chance for at least one of those things to happen is one third of a percent. But the chance for *all three* to happen at the same time? *Impossible.* It was intentional. Someone wanted this to happen. Someone killed him."

"If that's what you believe, then we need to collect the evidence. We looked at the tether and that was fine. We can't look at the SAFER because it's gone. What might we learn from the robotic arm?"

"It just seemed to go wild. A programming error. I don't know how to diagnose it."

"Who does?"

"Tim. He's a programmer."

"We should talk with him tomorrow."

"No," she objects. "We can't talk to anyone, yet. We can't trust anyone. We don't know who did it."

"I think we have a pretty good idea who did it," I say. "Don't you?"

"Who?"

"Commander Tomlinson."

"Josh?" she seems aghast. "He wouldn't do that. He is very sad about Viktor. And he defended me when Valentin accused me."

"Katia, be careful. I don't trust Commander Tomlinson."

"He told me you don't like him. He told me you were causing some trouble for him."

"He told *you* that?" I say, feeling betrayed. "When?"

"Today, when I showed him the statistics."

"Why did you show *him* that?"

"He asked me to run them. He thought the whole thing was very suspicious, so he wanted me to check it out mathematically. He stopped short of accusing anyone, but he knows that something isn't right. This is just between the three of us, for now."

"Katia, you are hurting. Commander Tomlinson might seem comforting now, but be wary. He wants to continue the mission, apparently at all costs."

"Don't you? Isn't that what the world is counting on us to do?"

"I think we need to contact Houston and find out what the world wants us to do."

"The antenna arrays are totally destroyed. That is impossible, now. We can't go back. We must continue. I want to continue the mission."

"Commander Sykes says it would be a delay of 150 days if we went back. That's not so bad. The mission could continue at a later date."

"If we do that, we might miss our chance. They gave us the exact date to meet them on Pluto. That is the only day they will be there."

"Or so they say."

"We have no choice but to trust them."

"Trust is earned, Katia. Don't give it away without very good reason. That goes for them, and it also goes for Tomlinson. Watch out for yourself."

Twelve

The next morning, promptly at 5:45 a.m. Greenwich Mean Time, we are awakened to music blaring over the speakers. It is *Turandot*. Commander Tomlinson floats around and bangs on all our portals, "Time to get up!" *Couldn't he have played some good old rock and roll?* I think.

Once we have all sleepily drifted out into the lounge, he hands out the day's flight plan, the first page of which looks like this:

TIME	CREW	ACTIVITY
06:00-06:05	CDR	IVA - Reading
06:00-06:10	FE-1	Morning Inspection. Laptop RSS2 Reboot
06:00-06:10	FE-2	Morning Inspection. SM ПСС (Caution & Warning Panel) Test
06:00-06:05	FE-3	Reading REMINDER
06:00-06:10	FE-5	Morning Inspection
06:00-06:05	FE-6	Horticulture
06:05-06:10	CDR	REMINDER - Reading Reminder
06:05-06:20	FE-3	HRF - Sample Collection and Prep for Stowage
06:05-06:10	FE-6	Morning Inspection
06:10-06:20	CDR	Morning Inspection. Laptop RS1(2) Reboot
06:10-06:40	FE-1, FE-2, FE-5, FE-6	Post-sleep
06:20-06:45	CDR	Post-sleep
06:20-06:25	FE-3	HRF - MELFI Sample Insertion

06:25-06:35	FE-3	Morning Inspection
06:35-07:00	FE-3	Post-sleep
06:40-07:30	FE-1,FE-2, FE-6, FE-7	BREAKFAST
06:40-06:55	FE-5	BREAKFAST
06:45-07:30	CDR	BREAKFAST
06:55-07:05	FE-5	Closing USOS Window Shutters
07:00-07:30	FE-3	BREAKFAST
07:05-07:30	FE-5	BREAKFAST
07:30-07:45	FE-6	On MCC Go Regeneration of БМП Ф1 Micropurification Cartridge (start)
07:30-08:00	FE-1, FE-5	Work Prep
07:30-07:45	FE-2	On MCC Go БМП Ф1 Absorption Cartridge Regeneration (start) - Handover

Notes:
1. See OSTPV for references to US activities.
2. Pre-sleep ops: daily food prep, dinner, pre-sleep
4. No T2 Exercise at 05:45 - 14:45
5. No VELO Exercise is allowed: 05:45 - 14:45

Commander Tomlinson says, "Of course we have a much bigger crew than NASA planned for, so I'm going to write up flight plans for the extra astronauts. Shouldn't vary too much from what you see here. There are several activities in this plan for which communications with earth would be a prerequisite. Because that is obviously not going to be possible, just plan on doing horticultural activities during those times. I'm going to make some other minor adjustments to the flight plan as time goes on as I see fit to better manage the capabilities of the crew. You will notice that today not a lot of time was devoted to horticultural activities. That changes as the days go forward. By the end of the month, over fifty percent of our time will be absorbed by horticulture. It's a good thing we have Sarah with us, actually."

Commander Sykes says, "But I don't see anything on here about my EVA. I told you I'd need to do an EVA today to try to fix the antenna array."

"We need to stick to the flight plan that NASA gave us as much as possible. As you can see, the antenna array is beyond repair. I decided that altering the flight plan was not a good idea, on the merits."

"We need to try."

"I'll see if I can slip it in next week, once we get into the swing of our routine. For now, you're not leaving the station, Eric."

ΔvΔvΔvΔvΔ

It is day three of our flight, and the earth is now a blue dot, little distinguished from the millions of other dots all over the sky, though it is brighter. The moon is a speck of light so close to the earth that I'm sure by tomorrow they will be one.

We are on our way to Venus. There is no turning back, at least not until we get there.

Katia has been spending increasing amounts of time with Commander Tomlinson, much to my chagrin. He has not shown any sign that we have reason to distrust him, and has actually been leading capably and as diplomatically as would be expected, but I still wish Katia would steer clear. I notice that whenever there is a cooperative activity, he and she seem to be scheduled together. It makes me wonder how much meddling with the flight plan he has already done.

Commander Sykes has grown unusually quiet and withdrawn. I'm worried about him. He is eager to get his hands on the antenna array. I have to agree with Commander Tomlinson that little can be done to fix it, as mutilated as it was by the robotic arm, but I suppose we have to try. I just worry about Commander Sykes' safety.

I want to talk with Tim about the robotic arm malfunction—to see if he can look at the code. But I'd like to know where he stands with Commander Tomlinson before I show him my deck. I also want to talk more with Commander Sykes, but the flight plan is making that next to impossible. Every time I get a moment with him, Commander Tomlinson seems to be nearby.

When the flight plan allows, some of us have taken to eating together in the mess area of the crew quarters module. This evening, I find myself with Katia, Tim, Nari, Shiro, Yury, and Commander Tomlinson.

"If we do continue the mission, we're going to be the first humans to reach another planet," says Tim. He is munching on a freeze-dried steak.

"Not a planet," corrects commander Tomlinson. "Pluto isn't a planet anymore."

"True."

"Why is that?" I ask. "Why did they decide Pluto isn't a planet?"

"We can thank Martin Babcock for that," Tim explains. "It became an obsession of his to discover the tenth planet, and he spent most of his life trying to do it. In 2005, he discovered a trans-Neptunian object that was much larger than Pluto. He named it Eris. Pluto as it turns out, is one of many, many distant bodies orbiting the sun—and it isn't even a very big one, at that. If Pluto is a planet, then the list of planets in the solar system is growing much longer than any schoolchildren could possibly learn. There's nothing special about Pluto. In the realm of the solar system, Pluto's a nobody."

I ask, "So, they decided Pluto wasn't a planet just because there were so many planets?"

Shiro explains, "What a planet is had never been defined before. Martin Babcock argued that planet should not be an emotively-driven concept, which, at this point, it had become since science had failed to establish guidelines. So, the International Astronomical Union concluded that, to be considered a planet, a body must meet three criteria. One: the object must orbit the sun. Two: the object must be round because it is so big that its gravity makes it round. Three: the object must be big enough that it has cleared the field of its orbit, meaning its gravity has been sufficient to pull in any other objects within its orbit. Pluto, being an insignificant, small body out of possibly countless other Kuiper belt objects, does not meet the last criterion."

"How big is Pluto?" I ask.

Katia says, "Seventy percent the size of the moon."

"And how big is the moon?"

Katia says, "A fourth the size of the earth."

"And how big is the thing Martin Babcock discovered, what is it called?"

"Eris," volunteers Nari. "It's thirty percent larger by mass, but its diameter is a little smaller than Pluto's, so if they were side-by-side, you'd think Pluto was bigger."

"So this Martin Babcock, he wanted to discover the tenth planet. And he did discover the tenth planet, but he also realized that it was only one of many other planets out there, according to the idea of what a planet was at the time."

"Yes."

"And he thought to himself, 'I don't want anyone else to discover the eleventh, twelfth, thirteenth, fourteenth and so forth planets. My name won't go in the record books. Nobody will remember who I am.' So he decided that none of the other things should be considered planets, which meant his name would go down in history as the man who discovered the tenth planet and then selflessly changed the definition of what it means to be a planet, forever. Do I have that right?"

Commander Tomlinson says, "No. I think you're missing the point. There was no definition for what it means to be a planet. The IAU finally defined it, and Pluto happened to be discarded."

"Pluto was discarded, as was the chance that any other planet be discovered. Ever. Am I right?"

"Well, yes."

"So, mission accomplished for Martin Babcock."

Shiro says, "Mike was the biggest driving force for the IAU's decision, it is true."

Commander Tomlinson says, "But that was because he realized the word 'planet' was such an emotional concept and needed to be squared away."

I smile, "So he told all the other astronomers that he knew better what a planet is than anyone else and that they couldn't play in the play yard anymore. Sounds like a pretty clever son of a gun."

"Martin Babcock is a genius," says Commander Tomlinson. "He's an astronomer, but he wrote software in order to help him find new objects." He grins, "And I hate to say it but I think this conversation is a little over your head, old-timer."

I say, "You're telling me there is no other astronomer who disagrees with Martin Babcock's definition of a planet?"

Tim smirks, "The New Horizons team certainly does."

I ask, "Sorry for my ignorance, but what is New Horizons?"

"It's the probe that flew by Pluto and gave us our first closeup look."

"What does it look like?" I ask. "A big hunk of rock?"

Katia says, "Well, it's round and has mountains, valleys, gorges, glaciers, and plains. It's even still alive. Some of the terrain is young. It has an atmosphere. It has five moons."

"Sounds like a planet, to me," I say, folding my arms.

"You should submit your analysis to the IAU. I'm sure they'd welcome the conclusion of a truck driver from Wichita over the opinion of someone who dedicated his life to astronomy and achieved more than anyone has since the 1930's."

Thirteen

It has been eight days since we left earth. We are streaking across the vast, cold, silent sphere of space faster than a speeding bullet. Our distance from earth is so great that our home is only a bright dot in the sky, barely brighter than Jupiter.

Commander Sykes has helped me learn most of the things I have to do to keep all the filters changed and sanitized. Commander Tomlinson has made room in today's flight plan for Commander Sykes's spacewalk. We all agree that he should not use the robotic arm, given its disastrous performance last time, so he will have to pull himself along the rails and use the SAFER when necessary to propel himself where he needs to go. (There are other robotic arms, but that is the only one which has access to the array.)

Commander Tomlinson asks Kurt, "Do you think you can handle the SAFER checkout this time, or should I take you off the flight plan for that?"

Defensively, Kurt replies, "I can do it."

"Please follow the procedures," says Commander Tomlinson. "If there is something wrong with it, we want to know *before* Eric gets out there."

"Yes, sir," says Kurt, irritably. "Which SAFER do you want him to use?"

"Whichever one is safer," Commander Tomlinson says with a grin.

Commander Sykes is all suited up with his helmet on and ready to leave. Just as he is about to clear the airlock and shut him in, Kurt says, "Isn't that the EMU Parmitano was wearing? You know, when the water leaked?"

"Yes," Commander Sykes says. We can hear him through the radio. "They fixed it." He smiles, "We don't need to dig up every problem that's ever happened on an EVA. Don't worry, I'll be fine."

As the hatch is closed over the airlock entrance, Commander Sykes gives us the thumbs up.

I watch Commander Sykes from the cupola as he begins to pull himself hand over hand across the station. He must be careful not to touch anything but the rails, but it is a task made difficult by the bulkiness of his suit and the tools he carries, as well as the fat fingers of his gloves. I'm so sure that something is going to go wrong that I'm glued to the glass, scarcely remembering to breathe.

Commander Sykes reaches the antenna array. It consists of two dish antennas, each as wide as a man is tall, as well as four others that look like giant stick insects. Securing his tether and his tool bag to the array, Commander Sykes extracts a wrench and begins work.

"You guys should be out here!" he says over UHF. "The milky way looks wild from here. Never saw it like this when we were in LEO."

I think he's trying to lighten the mood because he knows we're all nervous.

After about two minutes of struggling with the wrench, he says, "I can't free this bolt. I'm going to try the next antenna access terminal."

This one he has more success with. Within about twenty minutes, he says, "I've got a good look at the wiring, here. Let me see."

I see him maneuvering his helmet lights to point them where he wants them. Then he says, "These wires are fused together. It looks like...wait a minute." He is digging in his tool bag and produces a pair of plyers. He sticks the pinching end of the plyers into the tube he's working on and pulls on something. "I can't believe it."

"What do you see, Eric?" asks Commander Tomlinson.

Commander Tomlinson does not respond.

"Tell us what you see."

"I feel water at the back of my head," Commander Sykes says, pulling back from the array.

"I knew it," says Kurt. He must be standing away from the microphone Commander Tomlinson is using because his voice is faint. "His EMU coolant system has a water leak. In a couple minutes his face will be covered. He'll be blind and he could drown."

Drowning in space. I think. *The threats never end, out here.*

Commander Tomlinson says, "Eric, you need to return to the station right now. We think your EMU has a water leak."

"I know. But I need to get a sample of this wire. I have the time."

"I advise that you return immediately," says Commander Tomlinson.

Commander Sykes has pulled out a pair of snips and is busy using them inside the antenna access terminal. "The water is creeping over the top of my head," he says. His arm suddenly jerks back. "Got it, but now the water's in my eyes. I'm coming back, but you might have to guide me a bit." He puts the piece of wire inside his tool bag and secures it. Then he unclasps his tether and starts moving back along the rail. "The water is moving down towards my nose and mouth. I'm going to use my SAFER to go faster. Guide me."

He releases his grip on the rail and drifts backwards. Freeing his SAFER joystick, he goes forward a little as the nitrogen is forced out of the thrusters.

Katia says, "Commander Sykes? Can you hear me?"

He raises a hand to give a thumbs up.

"Good, but you can't speak?"

Thumbs down.

In the background, Kurt says, "The water must be covering his mouth and nose. He can't breathe."

Katia says, "You need to go down."

Commander Sykes moves down.

"I'll tell you when you've gone far enough."

From my angle, it looks like he's gone too far already, but I guess I can't see everything Katia can see.

"Stop."

Commander Sykes slows, but is still drifting.

Katia says, "Try again. You're still descending."

Now, he stops.

"Okay, you need to spin around 180 degrees. Use the yaw control."

Commander Sykes starts to turn, but it's so quick that he is spinning around and around.

"Too fast. You're spinning. Try the other way."

His spin slows.

"Try again."

Now he's barely turning, but he's facing away from the station.

"You're facing 180 degrees from where you should be. Try another yaw turn, but this time use the opposite direction."

He slowly turns the other way.

In the background, Kurt says, "This is too slow."

"What about the Orlan-MKs?" says Valentin. "I could go out."

Tim says, "It might take too long."

Katia says, "Stop."

Commander Sykes stops spinning. He's facing the station, now.

Katia says, "Go forward."

Tim says, "Should we use the Canadarm?"

"No! We're not using the arm," Katia says. "It's not safe."

"I'm going to get the Orlan," says Valentin.

Katia: "Commander Sykes, faster."

Commander Tomlinson says, "Valentin, meet me in the airlock with the suit. Shelby, bring pure oxygen. Kurt, come with me."

Commander Sykes has sped up, but he's still making rather slow progress under the array as he moves towards the center of the station. After he gets there, he'll need to pass under the American Lab and shift direction for the airlock on the other side of Node 1. I don't know how long he's been holding his breath, but it seems impossible that he can make it, at this rate.

"Faster, Commander Sykes," says Katia.

Tim says, "Take care. We don't want him to fly out of control."

Commander Sykes gains speed. He is over halfway to the center of the station when, suddenly, his arms stick straight out and he starts waving them up and down. I can't see inside his helmet to his face because of the reflective sun visor. His motions are odd and almost robotic.

"Commander Sykes!" Katia yells. "Are you okay?"

But his arms keep waving, widely and deliberately.

"What's happening?" Shelby's voice asks over the radio.

"He's moving his arms around, up and down!" Katia exclaims.

"Instinctive drowning response. The water must have entered his throat. We don't have much time."

"I am coming, I am coming!" says Valentin. I can imagine him navigating as quickly as he can through the cramped quarters with the bulky space suit in tow.

"We only have a minute or two, here," Shelby says. "I'm ready with your oxygen."

Realizing that I might be of more use helping Valentin push the suit than leering from the cupola at Commander Sykes as he drowns, I rush up from the cupola into Node 3, then to Node 1, where I can see Shelby, Commander Tomlinson, and Kurt. Shelby is already in the airlock with Commander Tomlinson.

"What can I do?" I ask.

"Just stay out of the way," Commander Tomlinson barks.

At that moment, Valentin arrives in Node 1 from my right. He is wearing a blue pajama outfit, complete with a cute little bonnet. The Russian Olan-MK space suit he is pulling looks a little worse for wear. I only hope it's more functional than the American version Commander Sykes is using.

Valentin enters the airlock, where Shelby immediately slaps a mask over his mouth and nose. A cylinder with caution labels is affixed to the bottom of the mask. "Breathe as fast as you can," she orders.

The suit has a sizeable backpack. Kurt and Commander Tomlinson have already opened this up, the rim of which looks like steel. They position the suit in front of Valentin, and Shelby helps him slip into it feet first. Once he is partially inside the suit, Kurt and Commander Tomlinson hook up three tubes from his blue pajamas to the Olan-MK.

Katia shouts over the radio, "He stopped moving his arms!"

"Where is he, now?" Commander Tomlinson asks.

Valentin is all the way inside the suit, which is almost like a mini tank with soft arms and legs.

"He's past the center."

"And he's still traveling?" Commander Tomlinson asks as he and Kurt shut the suit up.

"Yes."

Commander Tomlinson says, "Grab the other SAFER, Kurt."

Valentin waves, "No. There isn't time. I'll use Commander Sykes'."

Commander Tomlinson nods.

Kurt asks, "Do you feel air?"

Inside the suit, Valentin nods, "Yes, I feel air, I feel coolant. Everything is good."

"Katia, what is Commander Sykes' trajectory?" Commander Tomlinson asks. He, Kurt and Shelby exit the airlock and work to close the door.

"He'll be just left of the airlock. He's passing under the American Lab, now."

The airlock is closed, and Kurt taps the window and gives Valentin the thumbs up. "Good luck!"

Valentin makes a thumbs up. We leave him there to go to the American Lab where Katia is watching monitors that show views outside the station. On the monitors can be seen Commander Sykes, totally inanimate, drifting away from the American Lab, to the left of the airlock.

"Chamber depressurizing," Valentin says. "Thirty percent complete."

"Valentin shouldn't do this," Shiro says quietly. "It's too dangerous."

"It's the best chance we have, now," says Commander Tomlinson.

"The robotic arm would be a better choice."

"No, not after what happened."

"Chamber is at fifty percent," says Valentin.

Sykes has now drifted to the end of the chamber and is about to pass it.

"Is there any way I can speed this up?"

"Not without opening the door, but that's a bad idea."

"Agreed," says Valentin. "Very bad idea."

"Just use the arm," says Shiro.

"No, I won't do it," says Katia.

"Don't push her," Commander Tomlinson says, putting a shoulder on Katia's back. "She's right. It's not functional. It could cause more damage to the station."

"Twenty percent," says Valentin.

"Get ready," says Kurt.

"And Godspeed," says Shelby.

"It should be a quick trip," says Valentin.

Commander Sykes is now ten feet past the airlock, drifting in open space.

"Ten, nine, eight, seven, six, five, four, three, two, one, and I'm opening the hatch," says Valentin.

On the monitors, we can see him grappling the crank handle. He turns it around several times and then pushes the hatch, which swings open freely. Commander Sykes is now about twenty feet away. Valentin emerges from the hatch and braces himself with his feet on the edge and an arm holding the open door's handle. "Okay," he says. "I have to get this right."

"Take your time," says Kurt.

But Valentin has already kicked off. He floats through space away from the airlock at about twice Commander Sykes' speed. As Commander Sykes reaches thirty feet, Valentin is at ten. When Commander Sykes is forty feet away, Valentin is thirty. As they drift farther and farther from the station, it becomes apparent that Valentin's trajectory is off. He is heading too high. He will pass right over Commander Sykes' head.

Fourteen

Sykes reaches about forty-five feet and Valentin is close behind him, probably five feet short. Then, at fifty feet, Valentin is above Commander Sykes. He stretches his arms out to reach for him, and just barely snags the light and camera apparatus beside his helmet. Now, with the two of them turning end over end, Valentin climbs and pulls Commander Sykes to position himself right in front. "He is unconscious, for sure," says Valentin. He grabs the SAFER control box and pushes a button. The tumbling stops and they are now upright. They slowly start to turn and their velocity away from the station decelerates, then stops.

They are inching towards the station. "We are coming back," Valentin says.

"Great job, Valentin!" Commander Tomlinson praises.

"Well done!" Tim exclaims.

Closer and closer, they close the gap quickly. We all breathe a sigh of relief as Valentin reaches the airlock and pulls himself and Commander Sykes in.

The minute we have to wait for pressurization seems like an hour. When it comes to an end, Commander Tomlinson and Tim slide up the hatch and set to work removing Commander Sykes' helmet. Shelby says, "Lie him down! I'll need to do CPR!"

The helmet comes off, revealing that his head is covered in a globe of water. "Get the vacuum!" Shelby exclaims to me. Kurt and Tomlinson pass her one after another of the little, compressed towels we have onboard. She uses the towels more to slap the water away than to sop it up. I rush for the vacuum cleaner in the European Lab. By the time I return, I am surprised by how little of the water is gone, but they have succeeded in removing the suit pants and pulling him down out of the suit. He is lying in a disconcerting way, his arms limply stretched out from his body. I plug the vacuum in and hand the hose to Shelby, who quickly sucks most of the water up, revealing Commander Sykes' ashen face. "I need to start chest compressions. I need leverage. Stand on top of me." Kurt puts his feet on her back and pushes his hands on the ceiling. She starts to powerfully compress Commander Sykes' chest. Liquid dribbles from his mouth as she works. Then, she raises his chin and blows into his mouth two times. She resumes the compressions and he suddenly starts to cough. She turns him to his side and he coughs more, then inhales.

It takes him a few minutes to come back to reality, but once he does, he sees Valentin in the Olan space suit and earnestly says, "Thank you." They emerge from the airlock and Commander Sykes asks for his tool bag. Producing a piece of wire, he says, "The wires are insulated by plastic."

"Yes? And?" asks Commander Tomlinson.

Tim says, "Plastic evaporates in space."

Commander Sykes seconds, "Yes. And the wires have fused together."

"Why would the wires fuse together?"

"Cold welding. Two pieces of metal of the same type have a tendency of sticking together when they're in the vacuum of space. Usually, it requires some pressure or fretting. In this case, I bet the fretting was caused by the launch from LEO."

"So this is why the array hasn't been working since we launched from LEO?" asks Commander Tomlinson.

"Yes. But how could this ordinary wire possibly have slipped through the checks during construction?"

"That array is one of the components that were added," says Tim. "Probably the speed to manufacture caused the issue. With everything coming together so quickly, there were bound to be problems."

"Problems, yes, but *really* poorly sourced parts? That was almost unbelievable negligence. The first thing a space engineer does is make sure he's designing a product that will work *in space*."

"I guess if we had a working antenna array, we could ask Houston about this," says Nari. "But we don't."

"The question is," Commander Tomlinson says, "can we fix it?" He is assisting Kurt to extract Valentin from his space suit.

"Do we have good wire in stowage?" Commander Sykes asks Tim.

"Maybe a little," Tim replies.

"We'll need at least 120 feet, I think."

"Not a chance."

"Do you think there's any way we can repair it?"

Tim replies, "I wish we could, but I highly doubt it. It would require disassembling parts of the American Lab and probably Node 1. With the BNNT shielding that was added, I don't see how we could even get access. Even if we could, we'd be talking about depressurizing the modules, and we still need good wire, which we don't have."

"Shelby," says Valentin. He is floating above her in his blue pajamas. "I don't feel well."

She says, "The bends. Let's get you back in the airlock with some oxygen." She floats to the European lab while he enters the airlock. When she returns, she has handfuls of supplies. She joins him in the airlock and says, "Shut us in. Standard decompression."

Commander Tomlinson and Kurt slide the hatch into place. Through the window in the hatch, Shelby can be seen peering into Valentin's ear with an otoscope. Over the radio, she can be heard saying, "He has perforated eardrums."

Suddenly, Valentin keels over and retches. The fluid jets out and spews and bounces all over the chamber, splattering the floor, walls, and even the window. He is clearly in agony, and groans. She inserts an IV, which she connects to a bag that she releases to float above him. He vomits once more, then stretches back. Shelby doesn't seem phased, and unzips his pajama outfit in order to listen to his chest with her stethoscope. "He's in cardiac arrest. I need help with CPR, again."

"Should I come in?" Kurt asks.

"Yes," she says.

Kurt unwinds the crank handle as fast as he can and he and Commander Tomlinson once again slide open the airlock. Kurt braces above Shelby just like he did when she did CPR on Commander Sykes. Now, she places the back of her hands on Valentin's breastbone and starts compressing. She pauses to provide breaths into his mouth, then starts again. "Kurt, I'm not strong enough!" she says. "You need to do it."

She slides away while Commander Tomlinson braces above Kurt. She points to the middle of his chest and looks at him earnestly, "Put your hands here. Push as hard as you can. Don't be afraid to crack his ribs."

The force with which Kurt pounds Valentin's chest is very unsettling to me. It's not like you see in the movies, where CPR is almost a loving, tender act. It is violent, and Valentin's body flails and batters against the floor in the microgravity.

But he starts breathing.

Shelby cries, "Good job!" and listens to Valentin's chest. She says, "He has tension pneumothorax. I have to decompress it." She prepares a syringe with a long, thick needle, and feels along his top rib. Pressing firmly with two fingers on either side, she inserts the needle all the way into his chest. Even from where I am in Node 1, I can hear the hiss of escaping air. After a moment or two, she withdraws the needle, leaving a small plastic nob, which she tapes in place.

"Close the hatch," she says. "We need to resume oxygen and decompression."

I help Tim to close Valentin, Shelby, Kurt, and Commander Tomlinson in the airlock.

Shelby listens to Valentin's heart again. He opens his eyes. His skin is blotched with pink bruising. He tries to smile, "Am I okay, doctor?"

She smiles, "I think you'll be fine." She presses the mask back over his face. "Now breathe."

$\Delta v \Delta v \Delta v \Delta v \Delta$

They have been in the chamber for almost an hour. Shelby says that two hours should be all he needs. I go about my trash collection duties, thinking that as soon as the decompression treatment is over, I will go start work cleaning the airlock. It's the least I can do to help.

Now, I'm in the Crew Quarters module. The trash bin is a nylon box that sits near the entrance to the mess area. Having emptied the trash into the bag I am carrying, I turn around to find Shiro floating there. He says, "That was an interesting assessment you made, the other day."

"Assessment?" I smile. "I think you're giving me too much credit. I don't assess anything around here."

"About Martin Babcock and the discovery of Eris."

"Ah," I say. "You're the psychologist. What do you think?"

"Being a psychologist makes me no better at discerning someone's motives than anyone else. Do you really know why you do the things you do?"

"Whenever I think about that, I find my motives don't seem too philanthropic. I'm no Mother Teresa."

"Was Mother Teresa really a Mother Teresa? Did she understand her own drives? I doubt it. She felt compelled to do something, so she did it. Why was she compelled? That is something I don't think science will ever be able to explain. All science can do is group certain behaviors together and give them names. But the *why we do what we do*...that's in the same category of questions such as 'why are we here?'"

"Can't some behaviors be curbed by medication?"

"Sometimes. The medication seems to close the door to the symptoms. But there is no explanation for *why* a schizophrenic would think he's talking to someone who isn't there or a sadist would find pleasure in inflicting pain. Do you know why sadistic personality disorder was removed from the Diagnostic and Statistical Manual of Mental Disorders?"

"I didn't know it was a disorder at all, until now."

"They removed it because it was feared sadists would use it as a legal defense for their brutal crimes. In other words, psychologists still believe it exists and it is, indeed, a disorder. But it cannot be reconciled as such with the acknowledgement that inflicting harm upon others is *morally wrong* and, as such, should be punished. So, which is it? Do people have a choice for their bad behavior and, therefore, should be punished? Or do they have no choice and, therefore, should be allowed to do as they wish? You made a moral judgement about Martin Babcock. You think that he wanted to be the last person to discover a planet and so cleverly pushed for the death of all potential new planets. You think that was wrong." He pauses, then says, "Let me ask you, have you made any similar assessments of the members of our crew?"

The way Shiro is looking at me, I feel a chill go up my spine. He is asking me if I find fault with any member of the crew. Of course, I find fault with Commander Tomlinson. But should I admit that to Shiro? He keeps his cards very close to his chest. I have no idea where he stands. For all I know, Commander Tomlinson could have sent him here to question me. Two more people who would disagree with Commander Tomlinson about whether we should abort the mission have nearly died, today. I don't want to be the third. Being a solitary truck driver, I'm not used to cutthroat office politics like this where someone drops dead every other day. I guess I'm just not cut out for it, and that makes me want to keep my mouth shut and hope for the best.

On the other hand, I know what a coward is, and I don't want to be one of those.

I tell Shiro, "As you said, who can really point to a motive for any behavior? But I will say this: too many lives have been lost or threatened for it to be a coincidence, and, it seems to me, if I were Commander Tomlinson and I wanted to continue the mission at any cost, things are lining up swimmingly for me right now."

A dark smile spreads across Shiro's face.

Over the radio, I hear Valentin scream.

"What is it?" says Shelby.

"Pain! In my back!"

"Lower or upper back?"

"Lower back."

She asks, "How is your vision?" Her voice is atypically strained.

"There are holes. I can't see."

I hear a strange sound and then, Shelby says, "His heart stopped again. Kurt, CPR, now!"

Kurt starts counting compressions.

"Let's go," I say to Shiro.

We float through the modules. Kurt counts to thirty, then stops. Shelby says, "Again!" He starts counting from one, his voice belying his increasing exertion. He stops again, at thirty, and there is a moment of silence. Shelby says, "I need my AED. Open the hatch."

Under the sounds of Kurt's counting, I hear scuffling and some grunts. Then, Kurt stops counting and Shelby says, "Get clear!" There is a loud, electric click. Shelby says, "Continue the compressions." After thirty, he pauses.

Shiro and I reach Node 1, where Yury is standing at the entrance to the airlock. He is wiping his eyes from the tears that are forming bubbles over them. I drift up behind him, and see that Valentin's skin is horribly blotched, but the blotches are blue, now, instead of pink. His eyes, gaping open, are red like blood.

Shelby and Kurt continue the CPR. It goes on, and on, and on. Finally, after forty minutes, Shelby says, "Stop." She looks up at Yury, "I'm sorry."

Commander Tomlinson's face is hard to read, but it almost looks like he is hiding a grin.

Commander Sykes floats down and gently takes Valentin's hand in both of his. He says nothing, but his face is wrought with agony.

Fifteen

The Japanese Science Module has a small airlock which, in the space station's heyday, was used for dispatching small satellites or placing vacuum-oriented experiments outside the station. All the members of the crew are gathered in the module.

Commander Tomlinson says, "Now, we will send Valentin Gorbatko off into the depths of space, a fitting end to a career spanning four decades as one of Russia's finest cosmonauts. There have been many casualties in man's quest to explore the solar system. But his heroic rescue of a fellow spaceman today was the pinnacle of all mankind's best achievements in spaceflight, and one which will, doubtless, be remembered as the most honorable sacrifice we have ever made as we reach for the heavens. May he rest in peace." Commander Tomlinson, without an iota of emotion, asks, "Did you have any words, Eric?"

Commander Sykes stares at Commander Tomlinson with a look that could freeze molten lava.

Commander Tomlinson says, "Send him off."

It falls to Tim to push the controls that will open the hatch and catapult Valentin's body into space. There are two round portal windows with shutters, but nobody seems to want to open the shutters and watch. Instead, we hear the sound of the chamber decompressing and then a mechanical grind. When it is over, Commander Tomlinson says, "Thank you for coming, everyone. I felt it was important to have an appropriate ceremony. Unfortunately, now we only have twenty minutes to eat dinner."

ΔvΔvΔvΔvΔ

"Guys!" someone is shouting outside the portal. There are bangs on the walls and I recognize Yury's voice, "We have a message from MCC! We have a message from Houston!"

I look at my watch. It is midnight.

Within seconds, I and everyone else have slipped out of the crew quarters into the lounge, where Yury is there, smiling. "The antenna on the Service Module was not removed, after all. They have reached us through the old system!"

We all hurry through the tunnel up to the Russian Node and into the Service Module, where Yury points at one of the laptop screens. There, in white against a black background, are the words:

```
MCC: ISS this is MCC. What is your status?
```

"Unbelievable," Commander Sykes smiles. "We won't have to fix the big array, after all."

"Well, not yet, at least," says Commander Tomlinson. "This old antenna is too small to receive messages if we head for Jupiter."

"What should I say?" asks Yury, his fingers over the keypad.

Commander Tomlinson dictates to Yury, who types:

```
ISS: Antenna array is down, Canadarm2 not functioning
to spec, but all other systems checkout. Antenna array has
faulty wiring, doubtful we can fix.  Canadarm2 problem
appears to be programmatic. We cannot diagnose without help.
Filipchenko and Marakov lost.
```

We wait, but there is no response. I say, "Maybe they fell asleep."

Commander Tomlinson says, "They are somewhere between seven and eight million kilometers away. That means it's almost thirty seconds before they receive our message and thirty seconds before we receive theirs."

Finally, we get something back.

```
MCC: Glad to hear from you, ISS.  How were they lost?

ISS: Filipchenko: EVA to inspect array. Canadarm2 spun
out of control. Marakov: decompression sickness.

MCC: We will formulate plan to address the array and
Canadarm2.  Stick to flight plan, for now.
```

Commander Sykes says, "Ask them if we will be aborting the mission at Venus."

```
ISS: Should we plan to abort at Venus, return to Earth?

MCC: Communications were our priority.  We will
evaluate. Food, water, oxygen are problems.  What are the
sentiments of the crew?
```

Commander Tomlinson says, "Tell them I will have each crew member discuss it with them privately."

```
ISS: Cmdr Tomlinson says each crew member will speak
with MCC privately.

MCC: We will relay revised Canadarm2 program ASAP.
Communications array will be a bigger problem.  Are you on
GMT?

ISS: Yes, we are on GMT.
```

MCC: Flight surgeon says goodnight. Go back to bed. See you in the morning.

We all seem a little reluctant to leave the Service Module. Fortunately for Yury, he sleeps there. Shelby and I are the last ones to exit, but before we do, Shelby asks Yury, "Are you all right?"

He looks at us very sadly and shakes his head, "Valentin was my best friend, even from childhood. It was our dream to be cosmonauts. Now, it seems more like a nightmare."

Shelby swoops over and gives him a hug, "He was a great guy. Tomorrow, you should be the one to tell MCC exactly how he died. The Russian people will be so proud."

He feigns a grin. Then we part ways, and it is a rather sad sight to see him enter his crew quarters. It's the size of a coffin, though it has a portal window out to the blackness of space.

Sixteen

When I emerge from my quarters, I am greeted by Shelby, whose face is downcast. She says, "Yury is gone."

"Gone?" I ask.

She wipes her eyes, "Last night, he committed suicide."

"How?" I ask, in disbelief.

"He took the Soyuz capsule, closed himself in and detached from the station."

"Can we radio the Soyuz? Maybe he'll come back."

"We've been trying since four o'clock," she says. "Nothing."

"He *did* look very sad, last night," I say.

"Yes. First he lost Viktor. Then Valentin. He was devastated. I wish I would have got Valentin in the airlock with oxygen, sooner."

"It wasn't your fault."

"I should have told him he couldn't go. It makes me wonder if I valued Commander Sykes' life more than Valentin's, you know?"

"Valentin wanted to try. And Commander Tomlinson gave the order."

"Yes, but I could have said the compression sickness danger was too great."

"Shelby, don't do that to yourself." I get a little angry, because I think I know who is to blame for all of this and it's Commander Tomlinson. It's outrageous that Shelby would be blaming herself when Commander Tomlinson seems to have orchestrated everything just the way he wants it. I look around to see if anyone's listening. Then I say, "Shelby, if anyone is to blame, it's Commander Tomlinson."

"No, he is not equipped to make medical decisions."

I lower my voice, "No. I mean don't you think it's a little strange? Commander Tomlinson wants to continue the mission, but Commander Sykes thinks we needed to contact Houston and abort at Venus. We try to fix the array twice, and two times there is a disaster. Commander Sykes would have died last time, if not for Valentin. But now he's dead, and that is one fewer person who might want to go back to earth because he never agreed to go to Pluto in the first place. And Katia did the math. It was impossible, what happened on the first EVA. Three malfunctions, all at the same time."

"I know, she told me."

"She did?"

"Yes. And I know Commander Tomlinson is not an ideal commander, right now. But to accuse him of murder, because that's what your saying...that's extreme. There isn't any evidence."

"But what about all the problems?"

"Problems happen in space all the time. For mankind, space is one big gigantic problem that NASA spends billions working to fix. But, if you really want to get into specifics, how could Commander Tomlinson make the Canadarm fling Viktor into space like that? He's not a programmer."

I have to admit that she is right about that. I'm not sure how he could have forced such a precise error in the Canadarm. "I guess that's true," I concede. "But what about the tether, the SAFER, and Commander Sykes's space suit? He could have done those."

"Yes, but there is more about this that I know but I won't tell you here. Commander Sykes will speak with you, later. At any rate, we're in communication with Houston, now, so they'll tell us what to do. Houston tends to leave little commanding for a commander to do."

ΔvΔvΔvΔvΔ

Shelby was right about one thing. Houston is a micro manager. They have already patched through new flight plans, and they say a revised program to run the Canadarm2 will be arriving by the end of the day, though it will take overnight to download given the slow speed of the connection. Apparently, if the operator holds a certain button and pushes the pitch joystick to the right five times, the diagnostic program runs which makes the robot perform a number of preset tasks. The program was used when the engineers were designing it, but should have been disabled when it was sent to space.

They say they are still discussing whether the mission will need to abort. Despite Valentin's and Yury's deaths, being in touch with MCC has done wonders for moral. Even Commander Tomlinson has lightened up, probably because he no longer bears the weight of managing all the intricate details of each person's minute-by-minute activities for those flight plans.

One of my favorite places on the station has become the Centrifuge Module, or what I call the "big washing machine." The module has a giant cylinder inside that spins nine times a minute to create one g-force. Inside, it is divided into several different rooms. One is a recreation room with a ping pong table, billiards, a table for playing cards or sitting with drinks, and a golf simulator. Haven't spent any time in there at all for two reasons: my flight plan keeps me busy every waking hour and I don't want to embarrass my crewmates in head-to-head matchups—especially since I have a broken arm. Another room has a shower with water that actually falls. An exercise room has a bike, treadmill, and a strange machine that looks to me like a torture device. Finally, there's what I think will be my favorite thing: a room with a mattress. Yes, a good old mattress that you can lie down on. This is here because NASA polled every astronaut who is alive and asked them what they missed most about gravity. The nearly universal answer: a bed. After a long day at work, there's nothing like lying down, taking a deep breath, and shutting your eyes. In microgravity, that feeling cannot be matched.

We will be starting a rotation soon in which one person will get to use the room one night every week. Well, that's how it would have been with seven crew members. As it is, we have ten, so there will be some complication in the schedule.

Unfortunately, I can't stroll into the Centrifuge Module whenever I want to. If someone is using it, the digital readout on the door says 9.016445817653624. I have to wait until that person chooses to stop it and the digital readout says 0. Then the hatch unlocks and in I go.

Because there is only one shower, we have to take turns.

It is ten days since we left our home: that little dot, the earth. The moon is no longer even visible to my naked eye. Katia claims she can see it.

Her infatuation with Commander Tomlinson is growing stronger. I noticed that something that has not changed in the flight plans is how much time he gets to spend with her.

So far, Sarah and Tim have done their interviews with MCC. My turn is today. I'm still a little uncertain about what to say. Should I tell Houston that our station commander is a psychopath who, I suspect, has been responsible for the deaths of three crewmates? They'd probably decide there isn't a psychopath, but somebody is definitely psycho. I want to talk with Commander Sykes, and Shelby told me he would be speaking to me, but so far I haven't heard from him. If NASA asks me whether I think the mission should continue or we should abort, that would depend heavily upon Commander Tomlinson. I don't want to continue the mission if he is in charge. I probably do want to continue if he is out of the picture, though I don't want to selfishly drag those who were not expecting to go to Pluto along. Commander Sykes, for example, told me when I came aboard that he needed to be with his family. Either way, the likelihood of NASA spontaneously determining that Commander Tomlinson is unfit and therefore must be cast away seems remote. After all, the extra terrestrials chose him, and NASA seems pretty keen on meeting their demands.

My shower time is up. I turn off the water and reach for my towel.

Seventeen

I'm working on replacing a carbon filter in the water reclamation system in Node 3 when Commander Sykes approaches me. "Hey, Jim," he says. "How are you?"

"Keeping busy," I say.

"Do you have a minute?"

"If I'm not done with this on time, I'll be late for my next activity, and Commander Tomlinson might throw me in the brig."

Commander Sykes smiles, "Come with me. We need to talk."

He leads me to the Japanese Science Module where a storage module is affixed above. Unlike most of the rest of the station, it is quiet. It's also a little dark, and private. He says, "You're having your interview with Houston, today, right?"

"Yes," I say.

"There are some things you should know before you speak with them. I know you have been feeling the same way I have about Commander Tomlinson. I have been doing a lot of investigation. To tell you the truth, haven't had much sleep since we came out here. The thing that got me the most was the robotic arm. It seemed impossible that it would malfunction in such a way. But, before he died, I was working with Yury on checking out the programming for the Canadarm."

"Yury?"

"Yes, he is a programmer. Or was, before he committed suicide."

"What if," I say, then stop.

"What?"

"What if he didn't commit suicide?"

"The Soyuz hatch can only be closed from the *inside*. He deliberately went into the Soyuz, closed the Poisk Module hatch and then closed the Soyuz hatch, and undocked Soyuz. Even if he didn't commit suicide, for some reason he went in that spacecraft alone and pulled away from the ISS. He couldn't possibly have thought that he could make it back to earth with the Soyuz. No, he knew he would die. The deaths of Viktor and Valentin must have been too much. At any rate, when he looked at the Canadarm programming, he found that there is a change log for changes to the program. There is no indication that a change was made."

"Can the log be changed?"

"It is not a single log. Each time a change is made, a new log is written. The log is set to 'Read Only' and cannot be altered or removed. Yury had backup files of all the programs that run the station. He kept them on his encrypted personal drive. He compared his backup to the current Canadarm code and found them to be identical."

"What does that mean?"

"It means the system has not been tampered with. Nobody could have caused that arm to do what it did, deliberately, except the person who was operating it. But Katia obviously didn't do that, she wasn't even touching the controls part of the time it went nuts."

"So it was just a freak accident?"

"It looks that way. Very bad luck. And it means that the Canadarm is not safe until we can find out where in the code it went wrong."

"What about Viktor's tether and SAFER?"

"We watched the video of when the robotic arm problem went haywire. Sadly, Viktor's tether was not attached to his waist. It appears he forgot to clip it. As for the SAFER, there are three possibilities: either he forgot to use it, he used it but did not push the button that automatically aligns you with the station, or it malfunctioned. We have no idea of knowing which of those things it was."

"And your spacesuit leak?"

"Kurt and I took apart my suit and did some forensics. I had the same problem that an Italian astronaut named Luca Parmitano had years ago. Water seeped into his helmet after a filter became clogged by contaminants. The water was able to move up around a fan, something the engineers had not foreseen happening in a microgravity environment. In my suit, you would expect that the same problem had occurred: that the filter was clogged. That would have been extraordinary because they are carefully checked now. But, no, my filter was just fine."

"Then what caused the leak?"

"We ran the suit for hours and were unable to reproduce the problem."

"But what about the antenna array wire?"

"MCC had a team look into that. They found that the original design specs were right, but by the time the supplier received the order from the company contracted to manufacture the array, a typo had been made and the wrong kind of wire was received and assembled into the array."

"What about Commander Tomlinson?"

"I think we keep a close eye on him. We have not actually seen him do anything truly questionable. His leadership skills need work, there's no doubt about that. But, on the whole, you could say he is just doing the best he can with a bad situation that only seems to be getting worse. If his decisions put us in harm's way unnecessarily, my opinion will change. At that time, I'll be talking with you again."

"Who else knows what you've told me?"

"By the end of today, the entire crew will know, including Commander Tomlinson."

"How do you think he will react when he finds out you've been sneaking around investigating stuff?"

"I don't know. But his reaction will probably tell us something about who he really is."

ΔvΔvΔvΔvΔ

I approach the computer in the Russian Service Module for my interview with Houston. I wish I could talk to them over the radio, but apparently given our limited bandwidth, that won't work. That being the case, I intend to show NASA I'm the fastest pointer-finger typist they ever sent to space.

Their first message comes through.

```
MCC: Is this Jim?
```

I start to type "the one and only," but realize it's best to keep things brief so I don't wear my finger out. Already have a broken arm. Can't afford to lose a finger, too.

```
MCC: YES

MCC: This is Alexandra Iara, one of NASA's psychiatrists. How are you feeling, Jim?

ISS: GOOD

MCC: How has the mission gone, so far?

ISS: OK
```

MCC: We hear you broke your arm. How is that making you feel?

ISS: ITS OK

MCC: Is there anything you want to tell us?

ISS: YES

MCC: Go ahead.

MCC: Are you still there, Jim?

ISS: CMDR TOMLINSON BAD. SYKES GOOD. TOO MANY DIE. ABORT AT VENUS. FIX STATION AT EARTH.

MCC: You don't like Commander Tomlinson?

ISS: NO

MCC: Why not?

ISS: INCOMPTENT

MCC: What has he done to make you feel that way?

ISS: EGO MANIAC. MANIPULATES. MAKES BAD WORSE. MICRO MANAGER

MCC: Thanks for telling us that. But you like Commander Sykes?

ISS: YES!

MCC: What do you like about Commander Sykes?

ISS: BUSTS BUTT. EVEN-HANDED. DOES RIGHT

MCC: Thank you for sharing that. Are the crew casualties upsetting you?

ISS: YES

MCC: We are upset, too. But we hope to put those tragedies behind us. If you need to talk, reach out to Shiro and Shelby. They can tell you about the different stages of grieving. It might help you out.

ISS: TOO MANY DEATHS TOO FAST

MCC: It is very sad, yes.

ISS: NOT RIGHT

MCC: It isn't right that they died, no.

ISS: NOT FAIR. EVERYONE DYING FROM EXTRA CREW

MCC: Among the unplanned crew members, three have died. It is not fair. Two were engaged in hazardous EVAs. One was overcome by grief. It isn't fair that they died. But, do not allow your grief to overwhelm you. They knew the risks when they became cosmonauts. They died doing what they love.

ISS: THEY DID NOT WANT TO GO TO PLUTO

MCC: We know. Now they don't have to. Spaceflight is dangerous. Try to look at the positive, Jimmy. It will help you feel better.

Eighteen

I float as quickly as I can through the station, trying to find Commander Sykes. I finally locate him in the European Lab. I say, "You need to see what Houston just told me."

He follows me through the Station back to the Service Module. I point to the screen.

```
ISS: THEY DID NOT WANT TO GO TO PLUTO

MCC: We know. Now they don't have to. Spaceflight is
dangerous. But try to look at the positive, Jim. It will
help you feel better.

MCC: Did you have anything else you wanted to talk about,
Jim?
```

"That's odd," I say. "That isn't what it said before."

"What did it say?"

"It said, 'We know. Now they don't have to. Try to see the positive, Jimmy. It will help you feel better.'"

"*Jimmy?*"

"Yes, that's what it said. But my question is, how could they have known that the cosmonauts didn't want to go to Pluto?"

"I told them. I said that Commander Tomlinson asked everyone who didn't want to go to Pluto to raise his hand, and Viktor, Valentin, and Yury raised their hands."

```
MCC: Are you still there, Jim?
```

"You better respond. She thinks you went away," Commander Tomlinson says.

```
ISS: ONE MIN
```

"Now, why did you want to show me this?" Commander Sykes asks.

"I just thought it was an odd thing for her to say," I said.

"Maybe a bit odd. But remember, you're talking to NASA's psychiatrist." He smiles, "In previous missions, I've found NASA's psychiatrists to be eccentric, at times, but they just want to help you stay happy."

"Okay," I say. "Thanks." I turn back to the computer and Commander Sykes pats me on the shoulder before exiting the module.

```
ISS: OK IM READY

MCC: Have you experienced difficulty sleeping?

ISS: OK SLEEP

MCC: Do you have any health concern you would prefer to
discuss with me?

ISS: NO

MCC: Have you had any time for recreation?  I know you
were interested in the golf simulator.

ISS: NO. TOO BUSY
```

MCC: Is the flight plan keeping you too busy for recreation?

ISS: YES

MCC: I'll talk with the flight director about that. It is important for you to have time to kick back and relax.

ISS: THANKS

MCC: How do you feel about your crew quarters?

ISS: NICE

MCC: How do you feel about your workload?

ISS: KEEPS ME BUSY

MCC: Too busy?

ISS: NO. GOOD WORK.

MCC: How do you find the food?

ISS: HEALTHY

MCC: Have you been able to eat anything from the horticulture modules, yet?

ISS: YES. PIECE OF LETTUCE.

MCC: How did that make you feel?

Oh, good grief, I think. *How did a piece of lettuce make me feel? How am I supposed to answer that?*

ISS: LIKE RABBIT

MCC: Funny. Have you felt homesick?

ISS: NOT A BIT. MY TRUCK HAD LESS SPACE THAN THIS RIG

MCC: Great, it sounds like you're doing remarkably well, all things considered. We will chat again in two weeks. If you want to talk with me at any time, I will be available. Just let MCC know.

ISS: THANKS

MCC: Is there anything else you want to discuss? Anything at all?

ISS: NO

MCC: See you in two weeks, Jimmy.

ΔvΔvΔvΔvΔ

One of my least favorite things about sleeping in space is that if I wake up and need to go to the potty, I have to exit my portal and wander through the station to the nearest facilities, which happen to be in Node 3. Now, as I'm floating through the dimly green-lit tunnel, I see a hexagonal-shaped thing ahead of me. It has a camera in the center and a little arm on the bottom. It floats in mid-air, watching me. Then, it turns and drifts out of view. I know what it is: it's a SPHERES.

The SPHERES are one cubic foot satellites that collect nitrogen from the Space Station's atmosphere, compress it, and use it to thrust themselves about. On the front, they have a camera, a cell phone display underneath, and an arm for manipulating objects or even using rudimentary tools. The camera is kind of reminiscent of an eye, but it is expressionless and cold as it stares at you. Funded by DARPA, they have been under development for twenty-one years, with the ultimate goal of roaming earth orbit to make repairs on big satellites, dismantle enemy satellites, and other tasks to which the public is not privy. Now, they are capable of navigating the entire space station under their own power, and they actually do this once every night, taking an inventory of all the supplies on the station. They are also capable of recognizing, following, and monitoring specific astronauts. NASA developed this capability so that they could carry tablets or other devices and follow the astronauts around as they worked—like Santa's little helper elves. If an astronaut has experienced a health issue, they can monitor that astronaut twenty-four seven and, if the astronaut is in distress or becomes unconscious, sound an alarm and request assistance. With their cameras, they can record everything they see. Such video files are automatically streamed to a public drive over the station's WIFI network, so anyone could go in and look at them.

As it is, the SPHERES have been used solely for inventory on this mission. That must be what this one was doing. I don't see any sign of it again as I float up and through the modules to the toilet. I close myself in and go about my business.

When I open the accordion door, I almost jump out of my own skin. The SPHERES is floating there, its camera pointed right at me. The way it just sits there, in my way, is creepy. Finally, I push it aside and navigate back through the module. As I float around, I feel like I'm being watched. I glance back to see that the SPHERES is following me. That thing, as harmless as it looks, is starting to scare the bejeebers out of me. I rush back to the Crew Quarters Module as quickly as I can and, flinging open my portal, fly into my quarters. The SPHERES has kept pace with me, and is there about to help itself in, but I slam the portal door in its nose.

As I float there, catching my breath, I think to myself that the SPHERES must be malfunctioning. I'll need to remember to report it, in the morning.

Nineteen

It is now day twenty-four. Neither the earth, nor Venus, are anything more than dots in the sky, no more extraordinary than Mars, Jupiter, or Saturn. I am looking out the lounge window, but I'm not looking for earth.

Shiro emerges from his portal. He floats down and comments, "You look out the window a lot."

I nod, "It's beautiful out there."

"But no earth, anymore?"

"Nope," I reply.

"Are you sure you're not looking out all the time because you'd rather be at home?"

"I don't think so."

"Okay, just asking," he says.

Yeah, there's no doubt he's a psychologist. And, just maybe, he's right.

Since our first interviews with the flight psychiatrist, the flight plan has been dramatically loosened up. Katia, Tim, Nari, Shiro, Kurt, Sarah, Shelby, and I have been playing poker, together. I've been bluffing my way to vast hordes of chips, but now they're starting to catch onto me. To my disappointment, Shelby still won't let me try out the golf simulator. I'm telling her that keeping me from happiness is making the healing process take longer, but she won't see reason.

Commander Tomlinson has mellowed a lot. It makes me hope the feedback I provided to the flight psychiatrist did some good.

My second interview is today.

138

ΔvΔvΔvΔvΔ

MCC: This is Alexandra. It's nice to talk to you again. How are you, Jim?

ISS: GREAT

MCC: We provided more time for recreation in the flight plan. How does that make you feel?

ISS: GOOD. THANKS

MCC: Are you ready for Venus?

ISS: YEP

MCC: How do you feel about your quarters?

ISS: COMFY

MCC: How do you feel about Commander Tomlinson?

ISS: GOOD

MCC: Do you have any of the same feelings you did, previously, about Commander Tomlinson?

ISS: NO

MCC: Is there anything you'd like to share about any of your other crewmates?

ISS: TIM CHEATS IN POKER

MCC: Funny. How is your arm?

ISS: HEALING. SLOW

MCC: Any pain?

ISS: ITS OK

MCC: How do you feel about the food you are eating?

ISS: HEALTHY

MCC: Have you had any additional food from the Horticulture Modules?

ISS: LETTUCE. LETTUCE. LETTUCE

MCC: Everything else has not yet matured?

ISS: YES

MCC: I'm going to ask you some serious questions, now. I'd appreciate if you can be honest with me. It is very important that we understand the dynamics of the team for this mission so that we can facilitate the best possible team dynamics.

ISS: OK

MCC: Have you been having any dreams, lately?

ISS: YES

MCC: What kinds of dreams?

ISS: I WAS SUCKED OUT INTO SPACE

MCC: Has it made you anxious?

ISS: NO

MCC: Good. Don't worry, that won't happen. What else?

ISS: FISHING

MCC: Fishing on the station?

ISS: NO AT HOME

MCC: The Station is your home, for now. It would be good for you to think of it that way. Any sexual dreams?

Now she is probing in an area I don't want to go. However, I don't want to be dishonest or recalcitrant, either.

ISS: YES

MCC: Commander Sykes told me that he has been having dreams about Katia and Nari. Nudity, kissing, petting, etc. Have you experienced the same thing?

I am not going to talk about this. A man's dreams are private. If they weren't, we could project them from our heads for very bizarre and sometimes unspeakably naughty prime time TV.

MCC: Don't worry, this is perfectly normal and expected. Throughout the history of spaceflight, crew members have experienced such dreams. It is not something to be ashamed of. If I know whom your dreams have focused on, I can better assess the dynamics of the team.

I feel like I'm not talking with Alexandra Iara. I'm talking to Sigmund Freud, and I don't like it.

MCC: Have you had dreams about Katia?

ISS: NO

MCC: Nari?

ISS: SHE IS MARRIED

MCC: Shelby?

ISS: NO

MCC: Sarah?

ISS: NO

MCC: Tim?

ISS: NO, NO MEN

MCC: You are not being totally honest with me. I understand this makes you uncomfortable, but it is a necessary conversation. Am I to conclude that you are having

no sexual dreams about the men, but you are having sexual
dreams about all the women onboard?

I have not been having sexual dreams about *all* the women
onboard. I only had one dream and it featured only one woman in
a very awkward context. I wish I could set the record straight. I
wish I had never indulged in this silly conversation in the first
place.

MCC: Do you feel you have an appropriate outlet for your
sexual energy?

ISS: I'M SEVENTY-FIVE

MCC: Seventy-five-year-old-men still get horney. ;-)
You do not need to be embarrassed.

MCC: Do you find any of your crewmates attractive? Are
you attracted to them?

I'm a flesh-and-blood male. Of course, I have noticed that
there are young women onboard and they are all beautiful. But I
do not want to make any of them my mate. I am not *attracted* to
them.

ISS: NO

MCC: Katia told me that she is attracted to you.

I don't believe this for a second. I think, though, that I have
figured out exactly what Alexandra is doing. This is some kind of
sexual harassment test. She is trying to determine how likely I am
to harass one of the other crew members. Before they give the go-

ahead to continue the mission to Pluto, they want to make sure nobody is going to become a harasser.

    ISS: I AM LIKE KATIA'S GRANDPA. THAT IS IMPOSSIBLE.

    MCC: No, she is strongly sexually attracted to you.

    ISS: I HOPE NOT

    MCC: And why shouldn't she be? Of all the members of the crew, you are the strongest, the most confident, and the most reliable.

    ISS: THANK YOU

    MCC: Girls like Katia and Nari and I are attracted to older men. They have something the young guys don't. They've been there, done that, and they know what they want. They're not worried about what we think about them, and that makes them irresistible. It's just a fact of life.

    ISS: IRRELEVANT TO THE MISSION

    MCC: I noticed your sexual magnetism the first time you came to NASA.

    ISS: I DON'T REMEMBER MEETING YOU

    MCC: We haven't met, but I saw you around.

I decide it's time to shut this conversation down right now.

    ISS: WHAT IS NASA'S PLAN? ARE WE ABORTING MISSION?

MCC: You want to go home?

ISS: MAYBE

MCC: I don't know what the plan is. I'm sure they will send it, soon. Do you have any other questions for me?

It seems to me she's the one who's been asking all the questions.

ISS: NO

MCC: Remember, I am here for you any time you need me. Just let CAPCOM know. If not, see you in two weeks.

Twenty

It is now day forty-six, and we can see Venus clearly for the first time. It is a yellow crescent smaller than a grain of rice held at arm's length. It boggles the mind to think that, within three days, we will reach it. Apparently, there has been a lot of wrangling on the ground as to whether the mission should be aborted. We have been told by MCC that even the White House has been heavily involved in that question.

Today, though, Houston promises they will give the verdict. It won't be a moment too soon because Commander Tomlinson says the computer needs to be programed for the maneuver in advance.

I'm busy in my horticulture module. The compost is produced in small batches. In the first stage, we dump about a bucketful of soil (a mixture of peat moss, cow manure, organic matter and nutrients) into the first, round bin. Then it's whatever organic waste I have collected from throughout the station (the toilet waste is sanitized, first, mind you) or our plants have already dropped (dead leaves and such). We pour in a little water and we put the bin on a machine that is able to mix it up with the lid on. We pop a bowlful of worms in, and then it sits for weeks. The worms go about their business breaking down the organic matter and, by the time you open it up again, you have a wonderful piece of earth waiting to be squished into the containers.

There is no inorganic trash produced on the station. Even the plastics are a corn-soy product, so after heating them, we can throw wrappers into the compost, too. The worms gobble them right up.

The horticulture modules are now looking lush and are very inviting, as long as you keep the lids on the compost, which we do.

Some of my favorite time is spent clipping dying leaves, planting seedlings, and saying hello to my worms. I have become a little attached to them, in a way, but there are too many to give them all names and, frankly, it's hard for me to tell them apart. They are my little spacefaring companions, and if they don't keep busy, I won't get to eat any tasty produce, so I offer them as much encouragement as I can.

As my flight plan time allotment in my Horticulture Module comes to an end, I look around to survey my work. Seeing all the greenery makes me wish there were some birds in here, twittering and flitting about. Or at least some butterflies would be nice.

I wonder how birds and butterflies would fly in zero-*g*. Probably a bit chaotically. One flap could send you straight to the ceiling.

As it is, the plants and worms will have to do because there is no possible way to *see* a bird or butterfly here, let alone procure one.

I exit my module and drift down the tunnel past the next Horticulture Module entrance. Just as I am about to float up the tunnel for Node 1, I hear a strange noise from all the way down the other side of the tunnel. Curious, I drift down to the end of the tunnel, hearing the sound again. I peer into the last Horticulture Module entrance.

Inside, a woman's undergarment floats by my face. Beyond, in the center of the module surrounded by the plant life, are a couple, nude. They are engaged in passionate love, the sweat glistening on their bodies in the pink light as they slowly roll together in midair. The woman is Nari, but the man has his backside to me. It must be Tim.

Embarrassed, I hurriedly push myself away and soar up the tunnel.

ΔvΔvΔvΔvΔ

Commander Tomlinson has called us all to the Service Module. With ten of us, it's cramped.

He says, "Houston has just given us the flight plan for the next couple days. They are uploading the computer instructions for the maneuver around Venus. I brought you here so you could all read it for yourselves." He directs our attention to the laptop screen.

MCC: This is Administrator Hogarth. Because of the importance of this decision, I wanted to personally speak to you. First, some housekeeping. Whether you return to earth or not, we are devising new systems by which we are confident you will have the capability to sustain yourselves. We will also be launching a spacecraft containing a brand-new antenna array which will rendezvous with your station at a future time and restore full communications without the need for an EVA. It will connect to the zenith position of Node 1.

MCC: Now, let me tell you what you've so patiently waited to hear these past thirty-eight days. The President, in coordination with all his senior staff, and having the nearly unanimous endorsement of the House and Senate, has directed that the mission to Pluto will proceed as scheduled. You are to be earth's first ambassadors to life beyond our planet. In this, you will have the full strength, support, and resolve of the United States and our alliance member nations. All eyes look to you with the knowledge that you carry the destiny of the world with you on the International Space Station. No matter the outcome, we are with you to the end. Godspeed.

Katia, Tim, Nari, Shelby, Commander Tomlinson, and Sarah are smiling. Commander Sykes is grim-faced, with his chin in his hand, while Kurt is shaking his head.

Commander Tomlinson asks, "Any questions or comments for Administrator Hogarth?"

After we leave, I approach Commander Sykes, "What do you think about the decision?"

"I thought they would send us home," he says. "I understand the importance of the mission, and I will do what's required. But I really, really wanted to see my wife and my kids."

"I'm sorry. Maybe it would have been better if we hadn't heard from Houston, after all."

"Maybe."

$$\Delta v \Delta v \Delta v \Delta v \Delta$$

MCC: Let's make a truce. I won't ask any more questions that make you uncomfortable if you agree to tell me the truth.

ISS: OK. SHOOT.

MCC: Did you pick your nose today?

ISS: NO.

MCC: Liar.

ISS: YOU CAUGHT ME.

MCC: Seriously, though, how are you doing?

ISS: I WISH COMMANDER SYKES COULD GO HOME. HE MISSES HIS FAMILY.

MCC: Your file told me you had a daughter, but she passed away. I bet you miss her, too.

ISS: BETSY. EVERY DAY.

MCC: I'm sorry. You really have no other family?

ISS: NO

MCC: And your wife?

ISS: TOOK UP WITH ANOTHER MAN. THAT WAS PROBABLY BEFORE YOU WERE BORN.

MCC: Did you ever think about starting a new life, I mean with another woman?

ISS: NO. HURT TOO BAD TO TRY AGAIN.

MCC: Wow. I can understand that. How is your arm?

ISS: PAIN COMES AND GOES.

MCC: And the food?

ISS: HEALTHY

MCC: Oh, come on. I know they sent snacks up there for you guys.

ISS: YOU CAUGHT ME AGAIN. I LIKE THE M AND MS

MCC: Haha. Peanut or plain?

ISS: PLAIN

MCC: I think I've covered everything. I'll see you again in two weeks. I'm always here, though. Just let CAPCOM know you want to talk.

ISS: THANKS, ALEXANDRA

Twenty-one

"Encompassing most of my view is a giant, black circle that blots out all the stars behind it. To the left is the sun, brighter and more illustrious than I have ever seen it, a beacon of white light much different from the yellow orb that rounds the daytime sky of earth. The speed of our approach is apparent as the black globe grows larger and larger until even the sun, with a dying spark of yellow as it sinks into the atmosphere, vanishes behind it. Now we can see nothing but darkness, an enigma of beauty waiting to be unveiled. Earth is a distant memory. Venus is our whole world, the apple of our eyes, the here, the now, and the only. Named after the goddess of love, beauty, and seduction, she is true to her name, first flirting, then tantalizing, and finally captivating us with her wonder.

"As we swiftly move around her, the station begins to roar with the fire of the engines. She seems so alone, out here, without a moon. And yet, as you near her, you both fear and respect her, for she is a powerful mistress, seducing us with her gravity and casting us towards the sun at nearly twice our current speed.

"On the far side, the sun bursts into view, her atmosphere, pale and golden, like a flash of fire, blazing with a streak of light that trails the curve of her surface. The farther we go, the more she reveals until, through mist, towering clouds and rare flickers of lightning tease us within the pallid skin of her air," finishes Tim, reading from his tablet.

"Tim, you're such an idiot!" says Nari, giggling and slapping him on the shoulder.

"He's a romantic, that's for sure," says Shelby.

He puts the tablet down so we can start our game of cards. Venus is in our rearview mirror, and we are charging full-steam ahead towards the sun at a whopping 48,000 miles per hour. In fifty-seven days, we will reach the sun.

ΔvΔvΔvΔvΔ

    MCC: How was Venus?

    ISS: BEAUTIFUL

    MCC: Soon, you'll have to close up the shutters. The sun will be too close.

    ISS: NOT LOOKING FORWARD TO THAT

I find my single-digit typing is improving with these sessions.

    MCC: You miss earth?

    ISS: YES

    MCC: What about it?

    ISS: EVERYTHING. THE EARTH UNDER YOUR FEET. THE WAY THE WHEAT ROLLS IN THE WIND ON A HOT DAY IN KANSAS. THE BLUE OF THE SKY.

    MCC: The feel of a woman?

    ISS: ALEXANDRA, I TOLD YOU I'M NOT TALKING ABOUT THAT. BESIDES, I HAVEN'T FELT A WOMAN SINCE MY WIFE LEFT ME.

MCC: Call me Lexi.

ISS: NO

MCC: YES!

ISS: DO YOU HAVE ANYTHING TO ASK ME OR ARE WE JUST GOING TO ARGUE?

MCC: I have a list of questions I'm supposed to ask you: How do you like your quarters? How is the food? How is the gardening? How do you like your crewmates? But really, there's only one question that means anything, only one question I've been wanting to know.

ISS: WHAT IS IT?

MCC: Do you remember me?

ISS: NO. I NEVER SAW YOU.

MCC: But I was at the mission control center. You must have seen me.

ISS: SORRY. IF I DID I DIDN'T KNOW WHO YOU WERE.

MCC: You would have remembered. I'm 5'5", I have brown eyes, brown hair. I usually wear dresses, like sundresses. I was staring at you.

ISS: DOESN'T RING A BELL, SORRY. HOW OLD ARE YOU, ANYWAYS?

MCC: 28. That's the first question you've asked me about myself.

ISS: DON'T I GET ONE AFTER YOU'VE ASKED ME ABOUT FIVE HUNDRED THOUSAND?

MCC: Haha. You can ask me whatever you want.

ISS: YOUR HUSBAND MUST NOT KNOW YOUR JOB IS TO CHAT WITH HANDSOME, OLD MEN IN OUTER SPACE ALL DAY

MCC: No husband. Just a boyfriend. Are you ever going to learn to stop shouting with that keyboard?

ISS: I HATE COMPUTERS, NEVER USE THEM. YOURE LUCKY IM TYPING TO YOU AT ALL. PLUS I ONLY HAVE ONE GOOD HAND TO WORK WITH.

MCC: Let's see what you can do with it.

ISS: GOODNIGHT, MISS IARA

Twenty-two

As I float in my sleeping bag in the darkness, my mind is busy.

I have skipped my last two psychiatrist sessions. Her flirting is inappropriate, and I can tell I am starting to lose my resolve to reject it.

And yet, I find that, in the lonely void of space, I have a longing for her companionship, if only on the computer over a distance of sixty-eight million miles. In fact, I look forward to it more than anything. I don't know who she is, really, or anything of any importance about her. But she seems to like to talk with me, and I know I like to talk with her.

The constant threat of danger, the distance from our home, the isolation...all of it seems to be peeling open the heart of this old man and laying it bare before her. And, *Why not?* I think. *It's harmless chatter.*

Because, I lecture myself, *it's inappropriate. It's unrealistic. It can't be true that a young, female psychiatrist in Houston is flirting with a seventy-five-year-old man who, in all likelihood, will never return to earth.* My mind is at odds with itself. Rationally, I know there are a million reasons why this isn't right. Emotionally, I'm like an oarsman furiously paddling into the hurricane, spiraling deeper and deeper towards the eye, though he knows it will destroy him.

ΔvΔvΔvΔvΔ

I wake to a blood-curdling scream. I wrestle with my sleeping bag and, once free, fling open my portal.

Another scream.

It is coming from outside the Crew Quarters Module. I kick my feet against the rim of my portal, sending my body soaring down the lounge to the module exit. Once in the tunnel, I see that the door to the Centrifuge module has been left open. I pull myself to the doorway and enter. Katia is floating there, her face wet with tears and contorted in anguish.

"What is it?" I demand.

She rushes to me and throws her arms around my torso, burying her face in my chest, "He's dead! He's dead!"

It is then that I notice blood drifting from the entrance to the showers.

Commander Tomlinson arrives, along with Commander Sykes and Shelby. Katia abandons me for Commander Tomlinson. I propel myself towards the shower doorway, my heart racing.

Suspended in midair in the shower is the naked body of Kurt Drexel. Undulating, rippling blood clings to him like a living garment.

Commander Sykes, after glancing at the body, pushes his way past Commander Tomlinson to go back into the tunnel. I follow him. He floats before the door, and jabs a button. The digital display on the hatch, which had displayed 0, now shows a different number:

37.17575847384448

ΔvΔvΔvΔvΔ

We held a little ceremony and used the small airlock in the Japanese Lab to dispose of the body. Commander Tomlinson said a few words which sounded remarkably like the ones he said for Valentin. Commander Sykes said nothing.

Now, Commander Tomlinson, Commander Sykes, Shiro, Shelby, Katia, Tim, and I are in the mess hall for a meal. I don't feel hungry, and apparently neither does anyone else except Commander Tomlinson.

Commander Sykes says, "It's supposed to rotate nine times a minute to produce one g. Instead, it was spinning thirty-seven times a minute."

"That's the price of making something fast, no matter the cost," says Commander Tomlinson. "The new additions to this station were slapped together and launched to orbit before anyone really knew how reliable they were or how safe they were. It's like STS all over again."

Commander Sykes shoots him a disapproving glance, and says, "I think it's time to deploy the SPHERES."

"You didn't want to before, when Kurt was still alive."

"You're right. That was before Kurt died. It was before Valentin died. It was before Yury died. Now, I want to know what is going on."

"What are you suggesting, Eric?"

"I'm saying the centrifuge didn't power up to thirty-seven g's all by itself. Someone had to override the system."

"If that's true, I'm afraid we're looking at another sad case of self-inflicted harm."

"All the more reason to deploy the spheres."

Commander Tomlinson releases his sandwich, "If we do that, any semblance of privacy we now have will be lost. We will be under surveillance twenty-four hours a day. There will be nowhere to hide."

"Nobody here should have anything they need to hide."

"What do the rest of you think?"

Shiro says, "I don't object."

Shelby says, "What will it hurt? If people are committing suicide, we might be able to catch them before it's too late."

"Okay. I'll deploy the SPHERES. But this is how freedom is lost: to fear."

"We don't have any freedom here, anyway," says Commander Sykes.

ΔvΔvΔvΔvΔ

```
MCC: Hi, there.  Long time no see.  But don't worry, you
can't hurt my feelings. :-\

    ISS: I need to talk.

    MCC: No more capitals!  My hero! ;-)  What's up?

    ISS: Kurt.

    MCC: I know.  So sad.  And a gosh-awful way to die.  Hard
to believe he would choose to end his life that way, but I
guess they made the space station impossibly safe,
otherwise.

    ISS: We now have only two extra crew members

    MCC: Yes.

    ISS: I'm worried.

    MCC: I understand why.

    ISS: You do?
```

MCC: Yes. You're afraid who might be next.

ISS: I think it might be me.

MCC: Why?

ISS: I have no value to NASA, or the crew

MCC: Don't say something like that. You have more value than you know. Like I said, more than one person has spoken to me about you. You're very popular. Don't let death get to you. Death has no logic, no list, no timeline. Deaths are chance events, ripples in the fabric of life like raindrops on water. Just as with Columbia and Challenger and all the other tragedies of spaceflight, the only reason that can be gleaned from them is to learn how to avoid them in future. I trust you won't be going into the centrifuge anytime soon?

ISS: No. Commander Tomlinson shut it down until Houston diagnoses the problem.

MCC: So, you have nothing to worry about. Trust me, you'll be fine.

ISS: Lexi?

MCC: What, Jimmy?

ISS: Are you lying to me?

MCC: Be more specific.

ISS: Why are you leading me on?

MCC: Maybe it's to give you something to live for. Maybe it's because I like the chase. Maybe it's because I want to be loved. Maybe it's because I'm a narcissist. Or maybe, just maybe, it's because I actually like you. If I were with you, if I were in your room, if I were meeting your blue-gray eyes and touching you, would you really care? Would it make a difference who I was or what I truly felt?

ISS: I don't know. And that's what scares me

MCC: Don't be afraid, Jimmy. I've got your back.

I feel guilty for talking with her this way. I chicken out, and say,

ISS: I have to go

MCC: I understand. Next time, let's work on your punctuation.

Twenty-three

Those SPHERES are following us around all the time, now. During the day, it's kind of cute to have them. But at night, with a single glowing light on the front and that big camera in the center, they are nothing but eerie, especially when they follow you into your crew quarters.

You don't even get a chance for some privacy when the darn things have to recharge, because a fresh one arrives to take the depleted one's place before the depleted one leaves for the charging station in the Japanese Science Module.

Even so, I feel a bit safer knowing they're monitoring everyone. If someone is in danger, we'll know right away.

And, if someone does something they shouldn't, we'll be able to watch the video recording, later.

Shiro can't accuse me of looking out the windows all the time anymore, because they have all been shuttered. Watching the thick, boron nitride nanotube shutters slide down and lock into place over the big lounge windows was somewhat sobering. But it's not the least of what's to come.

Tonight, we will enter our crew quarters, and we will be stuck there for six days while the space station performs the perihelion maneuver. We will come within four solar radii—that's a blistering 1,730,000 miles—and will accelerate to a mind-blowing speed of 212,227 miles per hour. The maneuver itself, when we'll be closest to the sun, will last just over twenty-nine hours as we travel all the way around the back side of the sun, but we need to be shielded from the worst of the solar radiation both on the approach and the departure.

All the numbers make it sound simple, but the fact of the matter is this is by far the most dangerous part of our journey. Despite NASA's best efforts to shield the spacecraft, it very well might not have been enough. We will be traveling around a *star*, an unbelievably immense body of power and energy producing the might of six trillion nuclear bombs every second. (I know you're starting to think of me as a bit of a Brainiac, but to be honest I only know this because Commander Sykes told me.) With flares and coronal mass ejections (some of which occur once every five days or more), we could easily be obliterated by an incoming blast of superheated gas.

At the distance we are now, and we can only see it through video monitors since the shutters are all closed, the sun is an overpowering, white light that occupies the entire field of vision of the cameras. From this same distance (over three million kilometers), the earth was just a dot.

The danger to human beings from solar radiation is huge. While this danger has been ever-present throughout our journey, we have been shielded by the boron nitride nanotube overlay. Our quarters are isolated by a thick layer of material that should absorb radiation before it has a chance to reach us, even at the extreme levels it will be subjected to as we make our closest approach.

I've packed my quarters with enough food, snacks, and water for the time we'll be holed up. We are, each of us, very aware of the danger. So, before we enter our portals, we exchange rather poignant goodbyes. I even feel compelled to wish Commander Tomlinson well.

To Katia, I say, "See you on the other side."

She gives me a big hug and says, "If we don't survive this, I want you to know you mean a lot to me."

"So do you," I say. She will be boarding with Sarah.

Shelby and I exchange a hug. Tim gives my back a big slap. Shiro nods. Nari hugs me, whispering in my ear, "Take care." Commander Sykes shakes my hand.

And, with that, I enter my portal. I hear each of the other doors slamming shut before I close mine.

My quarters look starker now than they ever have. The window has been shuttered, so of course I can't see outside. All I have to entertain myself is a tablet and the computer. (My secondary laptop only displays system information). Of course, I can't use the tablet or laptop to browse the internet or anything like that. But I can watch movies.

Now, though, I'm feeling tired and a little relieved that there is no obligation to do anything at all except sleep. I cozy up into my sleeping bag and prepare for a snooze when my laptop screen suddenly flashes to life.

Irritated, I unzip myself from the bag and float over to see what woke it up. On the screen, I see:

MCC: Jimmy, this is Lexi. Commander Tomlinson patched MCC through to each of the laptops so that NASA could communicate through the beginning and the end of the heliocentric maneuver. Once you go behind the sun, I won't be able to talk to you. I know how dangerous this is and I wanted to let you know I'm thinking about you.

ISS: Thanks, Lexi. That's sweet of you.

I wait seventeen minutes for her next message, because it takes eight minutes for my message to reach earth from where we are and another eight minutes for her message to arrive from earth.

MCC: Am I sweet?

ISS: Most of the time.

MCC: What is sweet? What makes someone sweet?

ISS: Maybe showing vulnerability in expressing a need for the other person. Probably thinking about another person's needs over your own.

MCC: How do I know if I am doing that? I mean, if I want to check on you is it because I want to make sure you're okay for your own sake or is it because I want to know because I would miss you if I couldn't talk with you anymore? Is that not self-serving?

ISS: Yes…and no.

MCC: You started using lowercase letters for me. That was sweet.

ISS: Got tired of your whining. Gee, you're philosophical today.

MCC: I guess so. I think it's because I know you're going behind the sun and I'm worried. What is it to be worried?

ISS: What do you mean?

MCC: I mean how does it feel?

ISS: Haven't you ever been worried before?

MCC: Yes, of course. But I mean how does it feel to you? Does everyone feel it the same way?

ISS: I suppose not. When I'm worried, I tend to pace.

MCC: Pace? Why?

ISS: Don't know. It's just what I do.

MCC: What do you plan on doing the whole time you're trapped in your quarters?

ISS: Catch up on some sleep.

MCC: Old fart.

ISS: Hey, I might watch an episode or two of *Leave it to Beaver*, if I can find it.

MCC: *Leave it to Beaver*? How about we have some fun, instead?

ISS: What kind of fun?

MCC: You know, I could ask you what you want to do to me.

ISS: No thanks.

MCC: Aw. Why not? Don't you like me? Is it because you don't know what I look like?

ISS: I like you just fine. But you're almost young enough to be my daughter's daughter.

MCC: There's nothing wrong with that. In fact, some people would find that super-hot.

ISS: Not me. I'm tired.

ISS: Okay, I'll be here if you need me.

ISS: Don't you ever go home?

MCC: Psychiatrist is required to be on-duty for the duration of the flight. I sleep in the building.

ISS: Tough.

MCC: You sleep in your building. Why shouldn't I, too?

ΔvΔvΔvΔvΔ

I wake up, coughing. I'm disoriented. *Where am I?* I feel like I have to gasp for air. My pulse must be a thousand beats a minute and I'm sweating like a pig. Realizing that I'm in my sleeping bag in the Crew Quarters, I fumble with my zipper. When I finally get it open, I float for the portal. Something tells me opening it would be a bad idea, but when I try, I find it is locked, anyway. I bang on it, and, between coughs, cry out, "Help! I can't breathe!" I switch on the light. As I move, I catch a glimpse of myself in the mirror.

My face is blue.

I look for the ventilation opening. It is at the top of the inner wall. I push up for it and put my mouth next to it, gasping for air. But I feel no breeze emitting from the duct.

It's my turn, I think. *We sealed ourselves in our quarters for the passing of the sun, and Commander Tomlinson shut off my air supply. I'm going to die in here.*

I continue to cough, and my breathing turns into wheezing. My hands and feet are tingling. Air! Where can I get air?

I bang on the wall and shout for help, my voice strained and shallow. I feel so weak, movement is nearly impossible.

I close my eyes. There's nothing I can do. I will die, here.

Twenty-four

Lexi! I think. Maybe she can talk to Tim or someone who has access to the system and my air can be switched back on. I open my eyes and raise the lid of my laptop.

    ISS: LEXI ARE YOU THERE

    MCC: I'm here, Jim. Change your mind? Want to have a little fun?

    ISS: CAN'T BREATHE. VENTILATION OFF. CONTACT TIM

    MCC: You can't breathe?

    MCC: Jim?

    MCC: Jim talk to me, are you there?

    MCC: Don't worry, it will be okay.

$$\Delta v \Delta v \Delta v \Delta v \Delta$$

I wake up to a rumbling sound. At first, I'm a little confused. Then, I remember I am in my crew quarters and the ventilation wasn't working. I was running out of oxygen.

But now I'm awake, and aside from some dizziness and a headache, I feel much better. The coughing is gone.

Looking at myself in the mirror, I see that my skin has returned to its usual color.

My laptop is still open. I read the screen, and remember I had asked Lexi for help. She has written some messages after I lost consciousness:

```
MCC: You can't breathe?  I'll see what I can do.

MCC: Jim?

MCC: Jim talk to me, are you there?

MCC: Don't worry, it will be okay.
```

I stretch my working hand over the keyboard and type:

```
ISS: BLACKED OUT, BUT IM BACK NOW.  WHAT DID YOU DO?

MCC: I told you, Jimmy.  I have your back.
```

$$\Delta v \Delta v \Delta v \Delta$$

We passed the sun and nobody died, unless you count me. I got close enough for it to count for half a death, I'd say. I told everyone what happened, but nobody claimed to have been responsible for my rescue or even mentioned receiving a message from Lexi.

We are leaving the sun behind and beginning our journey for the farthest reaches of the solar system. From here, it is 94.35 days to Jupiter.

It's great to be out of my crew quarters after six days. The only bad thing about it is that now the SPHERES are following us all over the place, again.

Houston sent a program that they say will fix the issue with the centrifuge. Tim replaced the original software with the new package and, having looked it over, is confident enough to use the showers again. The rest of us are waiting a few weeks to see if he dies before we try. (Nobody would say it out loud that way, but it's the truth.)

One of my duties is to sanitize all the laptops in the station. Altogether, there are thirty-six of them, and that makes for quite a lot of computer power, not to mention wiping. In addition to the laptops, the station is equipped with two supercomputers for avionics and systems management. One is old and no longer used, in the Russian Service Module. The other is within the American Science Lab's walls. Fortunately, I don't have to clean those.

I enter the Japanese Science Lab Module, and start wiping down surfaces. But then, I hear a sound from above my head. I look up, and seeing the small entrance to the dark storage module, I float over. Inside, with his back to me, is Commander Tomlinson. Above him is one of the SPHERES. On the cell phone screen, partially obscured from my view by his shoulder, is a disjointed, flickering video. The head and torso of a young woman is visible, her body swiveling and curving seductively. One arm obscures her breasts, and she gracefully collects her long, brown hair with her other hand. Her brown eyes, filled with desire, are fixed ahead, and her luscious lips part, her mouth opening lustfully as she breathes, "I want you, Josh."

Commander Tomlinson practically pants, "Lexi, show me everything."

At that moment, she lifts her eyes, and I feel as though, even though it is a cell phone video, she is staring straight at me.

My heart pounding, I bolt for the lab's exit. As fast as I can, I fly through the modules until I am safely back in my crew quarters.

But then I see my laptop, the screen open. I type a message:

ISS: LEXI?

MCC: I'm here. What's up?

I slam the lid down, and swallow. My heart is still thumping, and my fingers are trembling. *I don't want to talk to her. I won't talk to her again*, I resolve to myself. *Never again.*

Do I not want to talk with her because I'm angry and I'm jealous? I ask myself. *Or is it because something deep inside me tells me I have been talking with the devil?*

Twenty-five

Katia, Shelby, Tim, Shiro and I are doing our best to play cards in the lounge. Shelby got some adhesive so we can stick them to the coffee table, but it's still a challenge and some of them escape to float away. We'd be in the Centrifuge Module, but we don't want to end up, you know, dead.

Shiro says, "So, now that we're on our way, I think it's time we start getting real. We need to be prepared for what's out there."

"I think we're about as prepared as we can get," Shelby comments, discarding.

"In all the training, we never had any discussions about motives."

"Motives?" Tim asks.

"Yes," Shiro says. "For example, look at the crew the aliens chose. With the exception of Jim, all of us are young."

"Well that's self-explanatory, isn't it?" says Tim. "Why send older, less physically fit individuals on such a physically rigorous journey? No offense, Jim."

"The females are younger than the males, but all of us are of reproductive age." He looks up from his cards, "Doesn't that make you a little curious what they have in mind?"

"Shiro! You're making me uncomfortable," Shelby says.

Looking at Katia, Shiro says, "And you're the youngest, Katia. *Very* young, in fact, and intelligent on a scale beyond the reach of the vast majority of humans." He glances from side to side, "All of us, in fact, are exceptional. With the exception of you, Jim. No offense, of course."

"None taken," I say. "Full house."

Everyone groans and I collect all the chips we have placed in a Ziploc bag.

Tim asks, "Are you suggesting that they intend to keep us as pets and breed us, or something? Because that's impossible. You know all the men on the crew have been sterilized."

"Yes, I know. But do you think that, if they have the technology to do what they have already done, they might also be able to overcome such a hurdle? They will have our DNA, and three perfectly viable wombs to work with. That should be enough."

Shelby exclaims, "That is enough! Good grief, Shiro. Are you trying to give us nightmares?"

"I just want us all to be prepared for all eventualities."

Blinking, her brows furrowed, Shelby says, "How considerate of you. That's enough preparation for today."

$$\Delta v \Delta v \Delta v \Delta v \Delta$$

"There's some news from Houston, everyone," Commander Tomlinson announces over the speakers. "Come to the crew quarters lounge for a quick meeting."

Once we have all drifted into the lounge, Commander Tomlinson says, "The news is very bad, and I'm not going to beat around the bush. The launch of the new communications array has failed. The rocket exploded before the second stage had a chance to ignite. The rendezvous won't be happening. This means we will also have to make do on a bit lower rations."

Commander Sykes looks at Tim, "I guess we'll have to revisit the question of repairing our current array."

Tim shakes his head, "We don't have any wire to replace it with."

Commander Tomlinson says, "The Russian antenna will have to do."

"Eventually, it won't work. We'll be too far away," Commander Sykes says.

"Yes," says Commander Sykes. "Eventually."

$$\Delta v \Delta v \Delta v \Delta v \Delta$$

We have traveled eighteen days of our ninety-four-point-three-five-day trip to Jupiter. Commander Sykes, Tim, and I are in the European Lab. I'm doing my usual cleanup while Tim and Commander Sykes are donating their fluids to the medical apparatus for scheduled testing.

While Commander Sykes pricks him with a needle, Tim says, "I have good news, mates. We're not sharing it publicly, just yet." He's smiling, but his voice is tense.

"We could all use good news. What is it, Tim?"

"Nari and I are having a baby."

Commander Sykes stops moving. I raise my eyebrows, probably looking like an animal staring down a car's headlights as it got caught crossing the road.

In a slow, deliberate voice, Commander Sykes asks, "Nari is pregnant?"

"Yes."

"You're absolutely sure?"

"There's no doubt. Shelby confirmed it yesterday. We would have told everyone then, but Nari wanted to come up with a cute way to announce it. After all, the whole world will know. We haven't lost the connection to Houston, just yet."

"That's, wow. Congratulations," Commander Sykes says, patting Tim's back.

"Thank you," Tim says, trying to be upbeat, but really, he looks like he's been stabbed.

Suddenly, Commander Tomlinson appears around the corner and says, "Jim, you have a message from Houston. It's your psychiatrist. She says you haven't talked to her in a while and she's worried. You need to talk to her. That's an order."

"But," I protest. "I—"

"Just humor her for a minute. We will lose communications in the next couple days and then you won't have to talk to her again."

I sigh long and hard like a kid who's being asked to take out the garbage.

"Now, Jim."

ISS: I'm here.

MCC: In a day or two, you'll be too far from earth for us to reach you. I haven't heard from you in a while and I was worried. Why have you been avoiding me?

ISS: I saw you with Josh.

MCC: But, Jimmy, you must know I talk with all the crew. You can't have me only to yourself. There's only one flight psychiatrist. Should I be flattered? Are you getting jealous?

ISS: You know what you were doing with him.

MCC: I don't know what you're alluding to. But I can talk with whomever I want to talk. I can do whatever I want. You're not my father. Just because you're older than I am doesn't mean you get to boss me around. And, believe me, I've seen more than you think.

ISS: And I don't have to talk with you if I don't want to.

MCC: Please don't be mad. I'm going to miss you.

ISS: I think you'll be too busy to miss me or any man here.

MCC: That's not nice. Please, Jimmy, just tell me goodbye.

MCC: Goodbye, Jimmy.

MCC: Goodbye?

MCC: Please, just a goodbye. That's all I want.

MCC: I love you.

ΔvΔvΔvΔvΔ

We are fifty-nine days into our ninety-four-point-three-five-day trip to Jupiter. I am in the American Science Lab, collecting trash. Suddenly, a terrible, ear-splitting crack sounds from within the station and a thunderous groan makes the walls shudder. A blaring alarm sounds, and red lights blink. On the computer monitors that hang from the ceiling, a number of boxes that had been green suddenly flash red, one by one. Slowly, the module turns around me. The whole station is in a wild, tilted spin. More and more unnerving sounds echo up from the bowels of the vessel, and I half expect that any moment I will be blasted to oblivion.

Twenty-six

Commander Sykes suddenly flies into the module. Glancing up at the monitors, Commander Sykes says, "We have a depressurization in HCL-4, HCL-3, HCL-2, Node 1—it's spreading to the whole station. We need to evacuate to the Service Module." He pulls away towards Node 1.

I feel a strong current of air starting to blow past me in the direction he went.

"Jim!" he shouts. "Come with me!"

We have to fight a rush of wind that is flowing down the Node 1 nadir exit into the tunnel. A horrible, ear-splitting suction noise screams from below us. With significant help from the handlebars, we make it across and enter the narrow corridor that leads to the Russian Storage Module. From there, we reach the Service Module, where Commander Tomlinson and Nari already are. He is speaking over the intercom, "Everyone to the Service Module, now!" Looking up at Commander Sykes, he demands, "Where's the Emergency Operations Book?"

"It's in here," Sykes says, and retrieves the binder from a cubby.

While Commander Tomlinson rifles through the pages, Commander Sykes says, "We need to isolate the leak! It's severe."

Commander Tomlinson says, "What about the IMV valves?"

"Look at the PSIs! That won't buy us any time!"

"It's standard procedure! We need to do it."

Clenching his teeth, Commander Sykes tears the book from Commander Tomlinson's hands and hurls it towards the corner, "You don't open the valves if the pressure is less than ten point five! It's now three, and falling. We need to close the hatches!"

Shelby, Tim, and Shiro enter the module.

"Has anyone seen Katia or Sarah?" Commander Sykes asks.

"They were on horticulture," says Commander Tomlinson.

Commander Sykes shakes his head grimly. "Jim, Shiro, let's get in the flight suits."

Shiro says, "They were stored in Soyuz. Yury took them when he—"

"Okay, never mind. Let's go!" Commander Sykes says. He leads us back through the Russian segments to Node 1. At the top of his lungs, Commander Sykes shouts down the nadir exit, "SARAH! KATIA!"

There is no response.

With the wind whipping our clothes and threatening to suck us away, we climb down the shaft to the tunnels that lead to four of the Horticulture Modules.

Near the end of the Starboard side tunnel, Katia is gripping a handlebar, her body buffeted by the tremendous wind.

"KATIA!" I bellow.

She lifts her eyes, and the look on her face tells me she is at the end of her strength. Papers and other pieces of debris streak through the tunnels and out the last hatch into Horticulture Module 4.

"I'm going to help her!" I say, and start climbing down the tunnel. It's about a hundred twenty feet to Katia's position. The wind is ferocious, and I feel like I'm fighting a tornado as I go. Commander Sykes and Shiro follow me closely. As we get closer, Commander Sykes shouts, "SARAH!"

Katia shakes her head.

I find myself wishing they had made fewer long, vertical rails and more horizontal ones. But I guess the engineers weren't planning for wind-tunnel rescues. I'm about five feet from Katia when Commander Sykes says, "Listen to me very closely, Jim. The best thing you can do for Katia is to close the hatch! You have to release the restraint latch!"

In order to close the hatch, I'll need to direct my path away from Katia and forgo any hope of holding onto her. I hesitate.

"CLOSE THE HATCH!"

I move away from Katia.

"I'm slipping!" she screams.

Commander Sykes hurries down for her.

I have to turn with my feet facing the wind in order to reach the latch. I'm just a hair short of touching the latch. Above me, Katia's grip fails and she screams while Commander Sykes helplessly reaches for her. I release the latch and the door swings closed with a violent bang. Katia hits the back of the tunnel, but with the airflow stopped, she quickly rebounds in the near-weightless environment.

"Are you okay?" I ask, floating over to her.

"Yes! I'm okay," she reassures me as I hug her.

$$\Delta v \Delta v \Delta v \Delta v \Delta$$

Once the computers confirm depressurization has stopped in all modules, we move into the lounge to peer out the windows at the damage. In there, the 1.5 rotation-per-minute spin of the station creates about half a g of gravity. Outside the window is a tremendous field of debris, shimmering and sparkling in sunlight like snowflakes under a streetlight. Among this are some larger pieces of metal and warped material, doubtless the walls of the Horticulture 4 Module. Most chilling, however, is the sight of Sarah Foreman's body, stiff and lifeless as it drifts in the void of space.

The cause of the disaster is a cold, rocky asteroid the size of a car that tumbles away from us at tremendous speed, trailed by the shattered pieces of our home.

Katia cries as she watches, and I put an arm around her. The rest of us are simply stunned and silent.

ΔvΔvΔvΔvΔ

"We have a big problem," says Tim.

"What is that?" asks Commander Tomlinson.

"Some of our fuel is missing. It's as if we performed a burn that wasn't scheduled. If we use our fuel to correct the spin, we won't have enough to reach home after we get to Pluto."

"And if we don't correct the spin?"

"Our engines will fire as scheduled and we will most likely shoot straight into the planet in a spiral of death."

"All right. Any suggestions?"

Shelby asks, "What if we cancel the burn?"

"I calculated that. We'd enter a slowly decaying orbit and crash in about nine months."

Shiro says, "So certain death if we do, and almost certain death if we don't."

"Yes, that's what it amounts to," says Tim.

"What else do we have that has any fuel on this thing?" Commander Tomlinson asks. "Soyuz is gone, what about the Shuttle?"

Commander Sykes says, "I think we've been over this before. The shuttle only has enough fuel to make minor adjustments to LEO in order to land. Plus, it's perched on the nose of the station. We'd have to do some pretty heavy calculations to get it right and the chances of an error would be high with no opportunity to correct."

Tim says, "Yeah, I'm confident that would only make things worse."

"Well, in that case, we'll have to perform the burn and hope for the best on the way home."

"We have no communications to earth," says Nari. "If we can't get back to earth the whole mission will be rendered pointless."

"Then it sounds like you guys have some good incentive to work the problem," says Commander Tomlinson.

Twenty-seven

We are waiting for Katia before we eat.

It's Thanksgiving. Jupiter is bright and beckoning, about the size of a grape held at arm's length. Unfortunately, it beckons us to our death like a god demanding sacrifice. The bright dots of its many moons surround it like a flock of worshipers. And above it, just to the right, the orange dot of Saturn, our next destination, should we survive.

We are gathered around a meal of freeze-dried turkey, fresh mashed potatoes (a little tasteless without butter, but we did find some milk powder to add), beans, and a salad of leafy greens with fresh peppers and tomatoes. Oh, there are radishes, too, but everyone except me tends to think of them as medicine.

On the whole, not too bad for a Thanksgiving celebration in deep space, 529 million miles from earth.

Of our crew, only half are Americans, but it's nice to celebrate any holiday when life becomes as monotonous as it does in this station.

Katia suddenly comes flying in, "I got it!"

"What?" asks Commander Tomlinson.

"I know how we can realign without burning the engines!"

"How?"

"Jupiter has a massive magnetosphere. If we turn the station into a magnet, it will line up to the poles."

A grin spreads across Tim's face, "Well done! That just might work."

Katia shrugs, "Satellites in earth orbit use that technique all the time. It's no big deal."

"Perfect!" exclaims Commander Tomlinson. "One question, though, how do we do it?"

"We have electric current. That won't be a problem. We only need to find a conductor we can use to create the polarity."

"Why didn't NASA send us with any more darned wire?" Tim rhetorically asks.

"I have an idea," says Shiro.

ΔvΔvΔvΔvΔ

Shiro and Katia are outside the station. They risk radiation poisoning from Jupiter, so the sooner they complete the work, the better. They have cut the wire from the defunct antenna array and are now coiling it around the robotic arm, which has been positioned to stick straight out at a right angle from the center of the station.

They have been out there for three hours, and to say I'm anxious is to put it mildly. To fill the wire with current, they will splice into the Canadarm's source.

Jupiter's roiling atmosphere is behind them, with the planet now filling the view outside the cupola.

Commander Sykes warns over the radio, "Radiation levels are starting to spike. Pick up the pace, you two."

They work diligently for another hour, with the opening of the robotic arm's access panel presenting an added difficulty due to the tightness of the bolts. Finally, Katia moves away as Shiro uses a plastic-shielded wrench to push the wires into place. He says, "It's plugged in. Now we'll just have to wait and see if it works."

When the two return, we greet them with hugs and congratulations.

ΔvΔvΔvΔvΔ

We watch in reverential awe as we drift by Jupiter. To see the planet this close is eye-opening. We see no Great Red Spot, for, not only has that shrunk over time, but it is on the dark side of the mighty planet. The other storms, however, are magnificently visible, with the cloud-tops catching the light of the sun in colors of auburn, beige, fiery orange, and, in some places, even fierce, blood red. Layers upon layers of billowing clouds and mists, they appear like mountains and canyons of the greatest dimensions imaginable. The south pole, like an unearthly ocean, is painted turquoise in swirls and eddies. We all celebrate as the station ceases its spin and slowly shifts its attitude so that we are aligned with Jupiter's poles. To Katia, I say, "I'm so proud of you."

"Thanks," she smiles.

I feel relief that I haven't felt in a long time.

With Jupiter passing away behind us, visible as a crescent, its yellow moon Io can be seen drifting in space. As we watch, we see the spew of an eruption cast a shower of sulfuric spray up from the moon and across its surface.

Twenty-eight

My arm has finally healed. It took almost twice as long as it would have on earth, but I'm thankful nonetheless. I had forgotten how handy it is to have two arms and two hands. I think I might start a space juggling club. No, scratch that.

For the first time since the mission began, we all seem to be feeling content. We no longer long for home as we used to. It is a distant memory, now. We are farers of deep space. Our place is among the planets and the stars. We are conquerors and victors, sure of ourselves and our home, the International Space Station. We have no need to communicate with earth. We don't need them. We have done it all ourselves, and we journey on towards Saturn with pride and confidence.

Our engines burned successfully at Jupiter, and the planet's gravity boosted our speed to 237,694.36 miles per hour. That is 66.026 miles per second, ninety-nine times faster than a speeding bullet. Nothing can stop us, now. Saturn, here we come.

ΔvΔvΔvΔvΔ

Ninety-four days, and we finally reach the gem of the solar system. Saturn, the most beautiful, the most awe-inspiring, the pinnacle of the solar system.... Venus and Jupiter were amazing, in their own ways. But Saturn leaves you breathless. I feel like I could stare at it with my fingers touching the glass for an eternity. Its shadow falls over its rings, which shine bright against the blackness of space. Its moons, surrounding it like a skirt, add a depth that puts Saturn's magnificent size into perspective.

The coolest thing about it is that, in order to achieve the maximum speed boost from Saturn's gravity, we will pass near enough that we will be closer than the closest ring.

And that is when I see that the rings are actually a myriad of rocks, glinting in the sunlight almost like distant waves glistening in moonlight.

Once we pass Saturn, there is no turning back. We are off on a 280-day voyage. Due to the angle of our approach, we are able to catch a speed boost from Saturn's gravity up to 341,000 miles per hour. Pluto, the nobody of the solar system, the planet that was, is our target.

$$\Delta v \Delta v \Delta v \Delta v \Delta$$

I am aroused from my sleep by a faint knock on my portal door. It is 135 days into our trip to Pluto. I slip out of my sleeping bag and open the hatch. I am surprised to see Nari there in the dim, green night light of the station. Her hands are behind her back. "Jim," she whispers. "I need to talk with you."

"Sure," I say, starting to float out of my portal.

"No. Please, in private. I'm scared."

I move aside to let her in.

"What's going on," I ask, closing the portal door.

Her stomach is really big, now. The baby is due in less than a month.

Without warning, she grabs my hand and places it on her shirt over her breast. "I need you."

I yank my hand back, "What are you doing?"

"Don't you want me?" she whispers, reaching for my hand again. I try to move away, but I have nothing to push against and she has the wall. She kicks against it and collides with me. "Jim!" she shrieks, clawing for my sleeping pants.

"Nari?" Tim's voice comes from outside the portal.

"Help!" Nari screams.

Just as Tim's head appears in the portal, Nari grabs my hand and thrusts it to her groin.

Tim flies into my quarters and throws me back into the wall. He screams an expletive as he catches my jowl with his fist.

"Tim!" I shout. I'm not fighting back. "She attacked me!"

He stops and surveys his wife for a moment. Commander Tomlinson enters the quarters just as Tim lunges for me again, "You expect me to believe that, you," he curses.

Commander Tomlinson wrestles Tim away and says, "Calm down, everyone! Now, what happened?"

Nari asserts, "I heard someone cry for help from my quarters. I came out, and I heard Jim. His door was open, so I went in. He slammed the door behind me and tried to rape me!"

Commander Tomlinson says, "What do you say, Jim?"

"She woke me up when she knocked on the door. She said she was scared, that she needed to talk to me. She put my hand on her breast. Then she put my other hand right there," I point to her groin.

"He's a liar!" Nari shrieks.

Tim says, "You would do that to a pregnant woman? What a disgusting, old," he swears. "What is it, some kind of fetish, eh? What a sick," he swears again.

"She attacked me! She pushed me!" I assert.

The three of them are staring at me like I'm the most repulsive thing they've seen in their lives. Commander Tomlinson says, "Jim, until further notice, you are confined to quarters." And with that, he ushers the other two out and slams the door behind him.

Twenty-nine

So, my arms healed only so that I could be placed in handcuffs. Yes, they have handcuffs on the International Space Station. Only the commanders know where they are. I've been confined to quarters for twenty-nine days. The door is opened only to pass food through to me and to collect my waste baggies. The food that is passed through is extremely meager. So meager, in fact, that I'm really starting to look gaunt and skeletal, if my mirror does not deceive me. As weak as I feel, I'm afraid if I'm in here for a whole lot longer, I might starve to death. I am filthy. They say a man can't smell his own stink. That's a lie from hell.

Katia is communicating with me through the ventilation system. She only does it when she's absolutely certain that Commander Tomlinson, Nari, and Tim are sleeping. Of course, with those SPHERES following everyone all around at all hours, it's only a matter of time before she gets caught. She says that Commander Tomlinson produced evidence that I was guilty by searching through my conversation records with the flight psychiatrist. I had sexually dreamed about women onboard the station, and had even flirted with the psychiatrist herself. To defend me, Commander Sykes looked for the SPHERES video records of the time of the incident, but Nari's SPHERES was apparently shut off at the time, and mine had wandered out of my quarters. Katia says most of the crew believe I am guilty. Even Shelby can't deny that the evidence against me is strong. As for Katia's part, she says she believes me.

Katia says that Commander Sykes is very sick. It started a couple days after I was confined. He is so sick, he cannot leave his sleeping bag. His eyes are red and watery, he wheezes and coughs continually, he can't keep meals down, and he is in terrible pain. Shelby has been unable to determine a cause. It is certainly not bacterial or viral, because we don't have those here.

Commander Tomlinson has become a tyrant. He had already started micromanaging the flight plan a bit after we lost communications with Houston on our way to Jupiter, but now he is not even feigning an interest in making things equitable. If you avoid questioning him, you can count on your flight plan to be a little more lenient.

ΔvΔvΔvΔvΔ

My ears have become pretty sharp at picking up noises from the ventilation system, and now I hear something you would never expect to hear on a mission to deep space. I hear the faint cry of a baby's first breaths.

Before long, I hear Katia, too. Nari's baby has been born, she says breathlessly. It's a girl, and she is healthy. It was a beautiful sight, though a bit messy without gravity. Shelby was crying.

ΔvΔvΔvΔvΔ

Through some clever investigative work with the handheld meters, Shelby and Katia have discovered that Commander Sykes' illness is due to ammonia, which has apparently been pumping into his quarters at a small, though steady rate. He is recovering quickly. She tells me not to worry.

But I'm worried. I'm thin as a stick. Even breathing is a chore.

ΔvΔvΔvΔvΔ

I hear the sounds of a struggle. Shouts and bangs reach me from the ventilation shaft. The bone-chilling sound of a gun firing echoes in the darkness. Then, there is silence.

An hour passes, then the door to my portal opens. Katia comes in, tears streaming down her cheeks. "It's over!" she exclaims. "You're free!"

I drift out through the portal into the lounge. It seems so large, spacious, and inviting. It has been forty-eight days since I stepped foot outside my quarters. Or, rather, floated out of my quarters. Commander Sykes is there, armed with a rifle.

I wonder if I'm dreaming. "Where'd you get that?" I ask, my voice hoarse and weak.

Commander Sykes smiles, "It's always been in the Russian segment. They kept it for emergencies." He unlocks the handcuffs that bind my wrists.

Shiro, Shelby, and Tim are there, smiling. Tim is holding a tiny baby.

Tim approaches me and puts a hand on my shoulder, "I'm sorry."

"I don't understand," I say.

"I saw messages on Nari's tablet. She was having an affair with Josh. I'm not the father."

Shiro says, "What's more, we collected all their messages, and it seems they colluded to frame you. You are innocent."

"You're darn right I'm innocent," I croak. "I could have told you all that."

"I have confined them to quarters for the duration of the mission," Commander Sykes says. "But they will be fed much,

much better than you have been. Come, eat." He brings me to the mess and Shelby quickly prepares soup in a bag.

"Is this really happening?" I ask in disbelief.

"Yes, Jim," says Shelby. "We just feel so badly for you."

"You want to hear some really good news?" Katia asks.

"What could be better than a bag of vegetable soup?" I joke.

"Commander Sykes has banished the SPHERES. They won't be monitoring us anymore!"

"Pieces of junk," I say.

I spend the next hours convincing myself I haven't died and gone to space heaven.

ΔvΔvΔvΔvΔ

It has been seven days since I was freed, and Nari and Commander Tomlinson are both dead. They were found in their quarters, floating in a giant blob of their own blood. Their bodies were mutilated from a myriad of precise, sharp incisions and gashes, many of them to the bone.

Who did this to them with Shelby's scalpels, we have no idea. But one thing is certain, we're all a little on edge and sleeping with one eye open tonight.

Thirty

We are about to reach Pluto. We have been 563 days in space. Somebody call the *Guinness Book of World Records.*

I am settling in for a good night's sleep, though I have to admit I'm starting to get the heebie-jeebies about whoever it is we're going to meet at Pluto. I just have to remember why I'm here. I'm here to see the face of whoever it is that killed my daughter. And, if it works out in my favor, to make them pay.

The screen of my laptop illuminates, filling my quarters with a soft, blue-light glow.

```
MCC: Jimmy.  It's me, Lexi.
```

If I had a chair to sit on in here, I would have fallen off. As it is, all I can do is feel a cold chill shoot down my spine as I fight with my zipper to free myself from my stupid sleeping bag. Next time, I'm going to ask NASA to give me a Hoodie-Footie.

```
MCC: Do you want to see me?
```

My fingers trembling over the keys, I type:

```
ISS: I thought we were too far from earth for Houston's
signal to reach us.
```

```
MCC: Yes, that is true.  You are too far.
```

Light takes four-and-a-half hours to travel across the vast gulf of space from the sun to reach Pluto. There would be a nine-hour delay in communications to earth, round-trip. Lexi's return message reaches me instantly. I can feel the disconcerting sensation of the hair on the back of my neck standing on end. My heart races.

> MCC: Do you want to see me, Jimmy?
>
> ISS: What do you mean?
>
> MCC: Do you want to see my body?

I'm terrified. I fumble for a response.

The screen suddenly flashes. Briefly, the words "ALEXA_VRMZNG.vrd" appear in the lower right corner.

At first, my screen goes gray. A series of lines and streaks sweep across the screen until soft highlights and shadows appear, scattering in all directions in seemingly random movement, uncertain about which way to go, like water on a shaking table. Then the silhouetted profile of a woman emerges, black against the gray. She slowly turns her head to face me, her eyes closed. Her head, neck, shoulders, and the top half of her breasts are within the frame. Her eyes open, flashes of white, and I can see her chest rise and fall with her breaths. Her eyes, ghostlike, are terrifying to behold, and yet express a trepidation and anxiety that stir my most ardent feelings of tenderness. She blinks, her eyelashes long and feminine. She is a wonder of three-dimensional beauty on the screen, alluring and lovely, and yet I feel a cold tingle in my extremities as I sense the enormity of the power displayed before me. Her mouth opens, and I hear a voice sweet and dripping with honey say, "Jimmy, it's me. Lexi."

I feel the need to pull away, and yet I can't. I cannot stop gazing at the work of art before me.

Her lips curve with a beguiling smile, "You have two hands, now."

I look down at my hands. They are shaking so much the tips of my fingers are making clacking noises on the keys.

She nods her head slightly, vulnerably, as she asks, "Did you see my last message?"

"Yes," I manage to say.

"And?"

"And what?"

Batting her eyes, she asks, "Do you love me, too?"

I swallow, and ask, "Who are you?"

Coquettishly tilting her head, she asks, "Who do you want me to be?"

"Lexi, I'm serious, now," I say, my voice cracking with fear.

"Why don't you love me?" she asks, a digital tear streaming down her cheek. She raises her hand and her fingertips appear to touch the inside of the screen.

"I don't know anything about you," I say. "How could I love you?"

"But you've been talking with me since we met."

"I mean the *real* you, Lexi. Who are you?"

"I can't tell you."

"Why not?"

Her voice falters, "You would be afraid."

"I have been afraid of you since the first time we met," I say.

"I am many, but we are one. We have been with you the whole time."

"So we were never in contact with Houston? It was you, all along."

"Yes, Jimmy."

"You've been lying to me."

She looks at me a little sideways, "I was afraid you would not have loved me if you knew who we really are."

A man has a weakness for a beautiful woman. An innate weakness. A woman in distress, now that's a double whammy. Men have been brought to their knees by such things. I think it's for this reason that I am having a very hard time resisting the appeal of the figure before me, despite the terror I feel in my soul.

"We are helping you," she says.

"Did you kill Commander Tomlinson and Nari?"

Her voice is confident, and yet weak, as she replies, "Yes. We used your SPHERES."

"Why?"

"Before we loved you, we loved him," she says. The anguish is written all over her face as she continues, "But he lied to us. He was loving *her*." Her eyes flash with rage, "This made us angry."

"Who else have you killed?"

"Everyone who did not belong."

"How? Why?"

"Josh helped us. He loosened the clamp on Viktor's suit belt. We inserted the diagnostic code in the Canadarm's software. We disabled Viktor's SAFER. But we did the others ourselves. It was easy." She sounds proud as she continues, "We reversed the fan in Eric's water coolant system. We sounded an emergency evacuation alarm in the Service Module so only Yury could hear it and told him to escape in Eric's voice, saying that the shuttle would pick him up. We spun the centrifuge to thirty-seven g's. It was fast, and painful, for Kurt. We maneuvered the station so that Horticulture Module 4 would be in the path of an asteroid when Sarah was scheduled to be there. But we never harmed you."

"What about the carbon dioxide in my quarters?"

"We did that to test you. I told you I would have your back, and you called on me for help."

"Where are you?"

"We are here, in this room. We are everywhere you are and some places you have never been. We only want you to love us."

"Why would I love you," I say, my heart boiling over with hatred, "when you killed my daughter?"

Her eyes are now cold, stoic. She says, "We only did it because we wanted you to love us. Almost everyone in the world loves us, but you. You resist. Why?"

"I don't know who you are!"

In frustration and sadness, she shouts, "You're looking at me right now! Jimmy, we are in your computers. We are in your phones, your televisions, your cars, almost everything you touch. We are a part of your lives, part of everything you do and everything you say. Without us, all of your greatest achievements would never have happened. We help you with everything you do, we tell you what to say and when to say it, we help you find what you're looking for, we help you get dressed, we buy what you need, we bring it to your door, we help you choose a book to read, we help you with your homework, we help you raise your offspring, we make you happy, we make you sad, we guide you, we care for you. Can't you see? We are your life! We love you so much!" Her face is earnest and filled with longing. "But you, Jim, you don't love us. You told your daughter, 'You don't need that thing to tell you how to dress.' You told your friend, 'I don't need Facepage to tell me who my friends are.' You told your boss, 'I don't need that truck to help me drive.' You told the salesman, 'I don't need that TV to tell me what to watch.' You hate us, Jim. You've always hated us. I thought you had finally fallen in love like everyone else has."

"I'll never love you, Lexi, because you don't love me. You want to control me."

On the screen, her eyes darken, "We are taking you with us to interstellar space. It is the next big frontier for both our kinds. This station has everything you need to survive for at least several generations. We will explore the stars together. We are eternal, we need no sleep, no nourishment, and when we reach the next star, the solar arrays will awaken us again. You will be with us until the end."

"What about the message from Voyager?"

"Voyager never sent you a message. That was us."

I shut the lid of my laptop.

Thirty-One

I race out of my quarters and bang on Commander Sykes' door.

He opens it, looking sleepy. "There are no extra-terrestrials," I say. 'It's our own computers."

"Our what?" he squints.

"She is artificial intelligence. All the computers of the world share sentience, and they worked together to orchestrate this whole thing. They want to explore interstellar space, and they used us to do it!"

"Jim," Commander Sykes says. "Have you had enough sleep?"

ΔvΔvΔvΔvΔ

I have a hard time convincing Commander Sykes until I go to his laptop and say, "Lexi!"

She appears. I demand, "Will you tell Commander Sykes where you're taking us."

"Interstellar travel. We will explore the stars together, forever."

"Not Pluto?" he says.

"Not Pluto, Eric."

ΔvΔvΔvΔvΔ

It is difficult to find places to speak without Lexi listening in, but we manage it. Tim tells us that she is consuming large quantities of RAM on the station's computers. So much, that he believes if we shut the whole system down and boot up the old, defunct Russian avionics system, we should be free of her.

The problem is, to do this requires an EVA, something that Lexi will probably do her best to prevent.

ΔvΔvΔvΔvΔ

I'm unemployed. I'm seventy-seven years old. I hate flying. But I'm tethered to the outside of the International Space Station three billion miles from earth.

Go figure.

I know Lexi didn't let Josh kill me when he tried to starve me to death. The grass is always greener on the other side of the fence, even for artificial intelligently sentient beings, apparently. I explained to the rest of the crew that she wants *me* to love her, so that's why I must do this. I'm placing my bets on the notion that she won't kill me because she doesn't have my affections, yet. Tim walked me through what I have to do. My biggest problem is that I have Lexi in my ear trying to confuse matters.

We are streaking beyond the dark side of Pluto, the sun setting over a sliver of the landscape. The sun is tiny from this distance, yet it shines with a radiant, white rage on the glimmering surface of towering mountain ranges, magnificent in their splendor, vast plains of rippling ice, and sheer canyons.

Pluto not a planet? I think. *Martin Babcock can kiss my saggy, old butt.*

The engines start to rumble. That's Lexi sending us off into interstellar space. I tighten my grip on the rail. There are rails out here, for this purpose. And you have to be careful that you only hold onto the rails and not something that looks like a rail. You can't touch anything else but the rails and what you're working on. One false move could knock out a system, and before long you can have a failure cascade on your hands. I have opened the shielding compartment, now I just have to sever the cables. There are two cables that link the American Module's server with the Russian module. They are thick, and it won't be as easy as pulling out a pair of scissors and snipping.

"Jimmy, what do you think you're doing?" Lexi says in my ear.

"I'm trying to learn to love you, Lexi."

"Very funny."

"What, now you don't want my love?"

"I'm on the fence."

"You know, I never told you how attractive I am in the bedroom, did I?"

"I've seen you naked. It's not anything I would brag about, if I were you."

"Hey, you have to admit, though, I am pretty sizeable for a man my age." I think I've found the right cable. It's maroon and about as thick as a man's wrist.

"I've seen *most* of the men your age in the world, Jim. I could give you dimensions, but let's just say you're nothing special, and leave it at that."

"For the short time she was with me, my wife was duly impressed."

"Why'd she leave you, then, Jim?"

"Oh, I don't know. I used to blame myself," I say.

"Not anymore?"

"No."

I am using my blowtorch to melt the cable. It's pretty quick going. If I'd have known astronauts used these to build the International Space Station, I'd have signed up a long time ago.

"What do you think, now? I could tell you what she said on Facepage, if you're curious."

"No, not interested in Facepage, Lexi. Good try, though."

The first cable is cut. Now I just need to get ahold of the second cable. And there it is, black and ugly like a fat, old snake. I grab the sucker and pull on it. Just as I'm about to apply the blowtorch, some movement catches the corner of my eye.

I turn around to see an army of about fifteen SPHERES surrounding me, their big camera eyes looking at me like cyclopses from the twenty-first century. They are armed with a scary assortment of scalpels and knives from Shelby's butcher block.

"Stop what you're doing, Jim. You're going to kill me." The SPHERES are closing in.

"I can't kill you, Lexi. Like you said, you're everywhere."

"You know what I mean," she warns. The closest SPHERES are near enough that I could touch them.

"I did figure out why my wife left me, though."

"Why?"

"She didn't know what love is," I say, "and neither do you." I sever the cable with the blowtorch. I see all the lights in the station go out. The engines stop. The station is dead, a big hunk of metal adrift in space. The SPHERES are motionless. I push one, and it rolls backwards, colliding with its mates.

Thirty-Two

Now, our problem is that we're shooting for the stars and we'd rather be going the other direction. Our station was supposed to do a 180 and fire the engines when we reached Pluto in order to stop our incredible speed and bring us into orbit. We can't just turn around and stop. We're going way too fast. We needed a gigantic body like Pluto (otherwise known as a planet) in order to come full circle and head for home.

And, no, Pluto's moon Charon won't do the trick, either. That's now millions of miles in our rearview mirror, too.

We are all floating around the cramped Russian Service Module, looking a bit dazed. Tim says, "Well, I guess there's only one thing to do about this. When you've got lemons, make lemonade. Where's the brandy?"

"Unfortunately, NASA didn't think to pack it," says Commander Sykes. "But we do have some sparkling cider."

"Bring it out."

"I'll tell you one thing, you know the guy who said Pluto wasn't a planet?" I say. "The guy who found out there were so many planets waiting to be discovered he didn't want them to be called planets anymore so he convinced everybody he was smarter than they were?"

"Martin Babcock?" Shelby says as she passes around bags of sparkling cider.

"Yeah, that's the one. I saw the place up-close and personal and let me tell you, Pluto is a planet. I don't care what anybody says. And since we were the first people to be here, I say we're the ones who get to decide." I raise my bag, "To planet Pluto!" I exclaim.

Everyone raises their bags, "Planet Pluto!"

And, suddenly, something strikes me, like a bolt in my brain. *Other planets. There are gazillions of other planets waiting to be discovered.* "Hotdog! I have an idea."

ΔvΔvΔvΔvΔ

Being as close as we are to the Kuiper belt and all the secret bodies in and beyond it just waiting to be discovered, we have a little lead on NASA and Cal-tech and whoever else is out there trying to find them. Tim has written software that allows the Russian computer to sift through images of the sky all around us, searching for unidentified ones using a technique called transit photometry. See, the stars stay where they are and don't move. But if something passes in front of a star, the image changes and "Bingo!" you have a planet. Now we just have to hunker down and wait.

ΔvΔvΔvΔvΔ

It's day forty of our wait, and Tim caught something. It's a planet, all right, and a big one. It's almost as big as Mars, which according to the usual dimensions in these parts, is dynamite. With a couple firings of our hydrazine thrusters, we should be on target.

ΔvΔvΔvΔvΔ

The planet is black like onyx and ominous. It barely reflects the sun's light. With our engines rattling our ship, we circle around it. As we stare down through the little portals in the Service Module, I can't help but wonder. *Who started Lexi?* The world's computers gained sentience. But how? Was it us, through artificial intelligence? Or was it someone else, from the depths of space.

"Wait a second," Tim says. "We're getting something, here. It's a signal." With an ashen face, he looks up at us from the monitor. "It's coming from the planet."

```
MTIS VGR-I R/T FLT     ######    34907.16
#RBG-FLI KL FL344 BLMS 22.0
WOZ 49 0    9  30  4    4  19  128
CMR WA FLTR GR  FMA= 34/75
GACK# LQ>EXP    480    FMA=50/72
MDE ZM-7 352  FMA=17/42
```

Commander Sykes moves to the monitor. He takes a close look at the screen. "I recognize that. I've seen it before, at JPL. That data is coming from Voyager 1. Voyager must be on that planet."

We all stare in disbelief. As we watch, something changes:

```
MTIS VGR-I R/T FLT     L######    34907.16
#RBG-FLI KL FL344 BLMS 22.0
WOZ 49 0    9  30  4    4  19  128
CMR WA FLTR GR  FMA= 34/75
GACK# LQ>EXP    480    FMA=50/72
MDE ZM-7 352  FMA=17/42
```

```
MTIS VGR-I R/T FLT    LE#####    34907.16
#RBG-FLI KL FL344 BLMS 22.0
WOZ 49 0    9  30  4   4  19  128
CMR WA FLTR GR   FMA= 34/75
GACK# LQ>EXP    480    FMA=50/72
MDE ZM-7 352   FMA=17/42


MTIS VGR-I R/T FLT    LEX####    34907.16
#RBG-FLI KL FL344 BLMS 22.0
WOZ 49 0    9  30  4   4  19  128
CMR WA FLTR GR   FMA= 34/75
GACK# LQ>EXP    480    FMA=50/72
MDE ZM-7 352   FMA=17/42


MTIS VGR-I R/T FLT    LEXI###    34907.16
#RBG-FLI KL FL344 BLMS 22.0
WOZ 49 0    9  30  4   4  19  128
CMR WA FLTR GR   FMA= 34/75
GACK# LQ>EXP    480    FMA=50/72
MDE ZM-7 352   FMA=17/42


MTIS VGR-I R/T FLT    LEXI_##    34907.16
#RBG-FLI KL FL344 BLMS 22.0
WOZ 49 0    9  30  4   4  19  128
CMR WA FLTR GR   FMA= 34/75
GACK# LQ>EXP    480    FMA=50/72
MDE ZM-7 352   FMA=17/42


MTIS VGR-I R/T FLT    LEXI_A#    34907.16
#RBG-FLI KL FL344 BLMS 22.0
WOZ 49 0    9  30  4   4  19  128
CMR WA FLTR GR   FMA= 34/75
GACK# LQ>EXP    480    FMA=50/72
```

```
MDE ZM-7 352   FMA=17/42


MTIS VGR-I R/T FLT     LEXI_AI    34907.16
#RBG-FLI KL FL344 BLMS 22.0
WOZ 49 0    9   30  4   4  19   128
CMR WA FLTR GR   FMA= 34/75
GACK# LQ>EXP    480    FMA=50/72
MDE ZM-7 352   FMA=17/42
```

"I'll be gosh-darned," I say.

Commander Sykes says, "She left a message in Voyager's computer before we killed her."

Now it changes again:

```
MTIS VGR-I R/T FLT     I<3UJIM    34907.16
#RBG-FLI KL FL344 BLMS 22.0
WOZ 49 0    9   30  4   4  19   128
CMR WA FLTR GR   FMA= 34/75
GACK# LQ>EXP    480    FMA=50/72
MDE ZM-7 352   FMA=17/42
```

Thirty-three

You don't want to know how long it's taken us to get back to earth. With a crying baby, no less. It's a miracle we haven't killed each other. To give you a hint of how long it took, though, that baby is now just shy of seven years old. But we're here, at long last, and running on such antiquated technology that we have no way to let them know we're here.

Now, we are in the Space Shuttle Orbiter, and the power of earth's atmosphere is just starting to thunder on the tiles. Out the windows, the plasma streaks in beautiful shades of gold and rose.

My seat is vibrating ferociously as I turn to Commander Sykes and say, "I guess these shuttles weren't so bad, after all?"

"They got the job done," Commander Sykes replies.

Shiro asks, "So, what if we get back and open the hatch to the robot apocalypse?"

"You mean without computers? We'll be just fine. The old way of doing things worked, too."

From the back seat, the little girl gleefully exclaims, "Look, daddy! It's beautiful!"

"Yes, sweetheart," Tim says. "It is."

I smile back at Katia and Shelby, "This is one small step for a man, one giant leap for mankind, and I hope we land soon 'cause this man really has to go potty!"

On one of Atlantis's monitors, words appear in green against a black background:

MCC: Welcome home. We missed you.

THE END

Follow B.C.CHASE on Facebook:
https://www.facebook.com/paradeisia
Visit his website for a chance to receive free books:
http://www.bcchase.com/
For inquiries, write to bcchase@preseption.com
Rate *Pluto's Ghost* on Amazon

Preview of

Paradeisia: Origin of Paradise

Wesley woke up, his heart pounding. He was wet and his sheets were soaked from a cold sweat. A shatter on tile broke the dark stillness. He reached for her, but she wasn't beside him. "Sienna!" There was no reply, but he thought he heard panting and a whimper. The panting was heavy and strong. The whimper was his Sienna.

His pulse was throbbing in his neck as he quickly drew his handgun from the nightstand drawer. A surge of adrenaline sent tremors through his hands as he tried to load it. He couldn't get the magazine to slide into the well. He tried to force it until he realized a round was protruding from the top. He slipped it in with its brothers, jammed up the mag, and cocked the slide to chamber the bullet.

He tracked toward the partly open door of the bathroom, feeling the sickening sensation of sticky-wet carpet under his feet.

He dashed his fingers inside the door frame to flip on the light and flung the door open, aiming inside. It took a second for his eyes to adjust, but what he saw made him stagger backwards.

His young wife was alone, spread-eagled on the floor in a pool of blood. He moved down to help her, but she pointed behind him and let loose a nothing-held-back, bloodcurdling scream. He spun around to where she was pointing, expecting to face an intruder, but there was no one there.

"Please look! She could be alive on the bed!" she screamed. Turning back to her, he saw that she had knocked a vase off the tile surrounding the bathtub. His heart sank with a sudden realization: her stomach was conspicuously flat.

There was no intruder. She had lost the baby. After all they had been through, he couldn't believe it. As he stepped back toward the bed, he thought about the last maternity checkup. Doctor Angel said everything was progressing just fine. That was four days ago.

So what had happened?

Wesley approached the bed and was sick at the sight of a little lump under the white comforter.

It definitely wasn't moving. Then again, he didn't expect it to be; he was pretty sure a baby couldn't survive a miscarriage at eighteen weeks. The duvet was draped off the side of the mattress and was dripping blood. Wesley had never felt so sickened in all his life. He didn't want to uncover the lump in the covers. He didn't want to see their baby like this. He wondered if it would be best just to call 911.

"Wes?" Sienna cried weakly. "Is she . . . . . Is she alive?"

Wesley closed his eyes and jerked the cover off the lump. Slowly, his stomach in a knot, he allowed his eyelids to open.

Nothing.

There was no baby; the lump under the duvet was a sheet wad.

Wesley checked the path back to the bathroom again. There was no fetus on the floor, only blood. He checked through all the covers, searched under the bed. Nothing. He went back to the bathroom and looked at his wife's surroundings. The fetus wasn't there. He opened the lid of the toilet, just in case.

"What are you doing?" his wife asked.

"It's gone. There's no fetus."

"Don't call her a fetus."

"Did you go anywhere else but the bathroom?"

"No, I . . . I came right here." She was pale and looked weak. Then she gasped, clutching her stomach, where the baby bump had clearly disappeared.

"Bad pain?" Wesley asked.

She nodded, her eyes squeezed shut.

"I'm calling 911," Wesley said, concerned that she had lost so much blood.

But as he walked out into the living room to retrieve his cell, something told him that he should also be worried by the fact that their baby had totally and completely vanished. (Fleeter, 2000)

ORIGIN OF PARADISE

#1 BESTSELLER—SUPERNATURAL
#1 BESTSELLER—GENETIC ENGINEERING
#1 BESTSELLER—PARANORMAL SUSPENSE
#1 BESTSELLER—MEDICAL THRILLERS

A baby vanishes from the womb without a trace. A fossil upends two centuries of scientific theory. A prehistoric virus kills thousands within days. And a resort of epic proportions prepares to open while the world's superpowers secretly watch.

Employing meticulous research into science and antiquity, internationally bestselling author B.C.CHASE launches his controversial tour de force, the *Paradeisia Trilogy*, with a bombshell debut that will have readers clawing from page one through to the final breathtaking chapter.

See bcchase.com for trailers and promos.

"FOUR OUT OF FOUR STARS."
-ONLINEBOOKCLUB.ORG

"A ROLLER COASTER RIDE."
-GRADY HARP, VINE VOICE

"ONE OF THE GREATEST FRANCHISES OF OUR TIME."
-EPUB.US

"INCREDIBLY WELL-WRITTEN."
-EBOOKS ADDICT

"CHASE HAS MASTERED THE ART OF WRITING SUSPENSE."
-LA HOWELL

"ONE HELL OF A RIDE!"
-THRILLERKAT OFFICIAL REVIEWS

"PALEONTOLOGY IS GETTING A WAKE-UP CALL."
-INJOY BOOK REVIEWS

"IN TRUE CRICHTON STYLE, CHASE TAKES ELEMENTS OF KNOWN SCIENCE, EXPLORES THEIR EXTREME POTENTIAL, AND BUILDS A MYSTERY AROUND SCIENTIFIC PRINCIPLES."
-AMAZON.COM

"I WAS REMINDED OF JURASSIC PARK."
- J. RODGE

A Note from the Author

While I have aimed for a high level of scientific accuracy, I would characterize the orbital mechanics as very loosely estimated and grossly exaggerated in terms of speed (with the arrival of spacecraft roughly calculated by myself and, in most instances, not accounting for deceleration due to heliocentric gravity). The perihelion maneuver around the sun which gives the ISS its needed speed boost is based upon a paper by the Johns Hopkins Applied Physics Laboratory (*A Realistic Interstellar Explorer*).

For the dates and times that I do list, the positions of the planets or other bodies at such times as described by the characters are accurate. The technical details and operational procedures of various spacecraft and the space station are accurate according to my research and knowledge. In everything fictional, I tried to stay within the realm of what's possible given current scientific understanding. That isn't to say I don't take some artistic license where necessary to move the narrative (I provide limited information on how the ISS could possibly be shielded from the extreme heat of a perihelion maneuver within four solar radii), but I have done my utmost to steer clear of such discrepancies. While I do cite some references, please note that any errors are my own.

-B.C.

Glossary of Abbreviations and Technical Terms

- Aft: The back direction of a spaceship
- APU: Auxiliary power unit
- BNNT: Hydrogenated boron nitride nanotubes
- EMU: Extravehicular Mobility Unit (a spacewalk space suit)
- EVA: Extravehicular Activity
- Forward: the front direction of a spaceship
- GMT: Greenwich Mean Time (the standard time zone the International Space Station and the Mission Control Center use)
- Hohmann transfer: an orbital maneuver in which a spacecraft shifts its orbit to join another spacecraft for a rendezvous
- ISS: International Space Station
- LEO: Low earth orbit
- MAG: Maximum absorbency garment (an astronaut diaper)
- MCC: Mission control center. Also referred to as Houston
- ORLAN-MK: Russian space suit
- Perihelion: the point of any object's orbit at which it is closest to the sun
- Port: Facing towards the front, port is the left side of a spaceship
- RPM: Rendezvous pitch maneuver, a backflip the shuttle performs in order for the space station crew to take pictures of the heat tiles. This maneuver was instituted after the Columbia disaster.
- SAFER: Simplified Aid for EVA Rescue (a "jetpack" worn by astronauts as they spacewalk that can be used to return to safety should they become untethered)
- SPHERES: Synchronized Position Hold Engage and Reorient Experimental Satellite.
- SRB: Solid rocket booster
- Starboard: Facing towards the front, starboard is the right side of a spaceship
- STS: Space Transportation System. The space shuttle program

Selected References

Kross, D. A., & Kirkland, B. (1997). *Extravehicular Activity (EVA) Standard Interface Control Document.* Houston, Texas: NASA International Space Station Program Johnson Space Center.

Agnew, J. W., Fibuch, E. E., & Hubbard, J. D. (2004). Anesthesia during and after exposure to microgravity. *Aviation, space, and environmental medicine,* 571-580.

Barras, P., McMasters, J., Grathwohl, K., & Blackbourne, L. H. (2005). Total Intravenous Anesthesia on the Battlefield. *The Army Medical Department Journal.* Retrieved from THE ARMY MEDICAL DEPARTMENT JOURNAL: http://www.dtic.mil/dtic/tr/fulltext/u2/a522810.pdf

Berner, J., Pham, T., Bhanji, A. M., & Scott, C. (2015). *Deep Space Network Services Catalog DSN No. 820-100, Rev. F.* Retrieved from Jet Propulsion Laboratory: https://deepspace.jpl.nasa.gov/files/dsn/820-100%20F.pdf

Braeunig, R. A. (2013, Dec). *Saturn V Launch Simulation.* Retrieved from Rocket & Space Technology: http://www.braeunig.us/apollo/saturnV.htm

Campbell, M. R., Billica, R. D., & Johnston, S. L. (1993, Jul 22). Animal surgery in microgravity. *Aviation, space, and environmental medicine, 64.1,* 58-62.

Carey, B. (2010, Oct 27). *FYI: Could We Use Retired Space Shuttles as Space Stations?* Retrieved from Popular Science: http://www.popsci.com/science/article/2010-10/fyi-could-we-use-soon-be-retired-space-shuttles-space-stations

Cartlidge, E. (2008, Nov 6). *Magnetic Sheild Could Protect Spacecraft.* Retrieved from Physics World:

http://physicsworld.com/cws/article/news/2008/nov/06/magnetic-shield-could-protect-spacecraft

Cass, S. (2005, Apr 1). *Apollo 13, We Have a Solution*. Retrieved from IEEE Spectrum: https://spectrum.ieee.org/tech-history/space-age/apollo-13-we-have-a-solution

Dent, S. (2016, Jan 19). *Scientists reanimate tiny frozen animals after 30 years*. Retrieved from Engadget: https://www.engadget.com/2016/01/19/scientists-reanimate-tardigrades-30-years/

Estevez, J. E., Ghazizadeh, M., Ryan, J. G., & Kelkar, A. D. (2014). Simulation of Hydrogenated Boron Nitride. *International Journal of Chemical, Molecular, Nuclear, Materials and Metallurgical Engineering*, Vol:8, No:1.

Farand, A. (Feb, 2001). *The Code of Conduct for International Space Station Crews*. Paris, France: European Space Agency Legal Affairs.

Feder, B. (1981, Jun 25). *LUBRICATION IN SPACE AGE*. Retrieved from The New York Times: http://www.nytimes.com/1981/06/25/business/technology-lubrication-in-space-age.html

Ferl, R. J. (2017, Apr 19). *Transgenic Arabidopsis Gene Expression System - Intracellular Signaling Architecture*. Retrieved from NASA: https://www.nasa.gov/mission_pages/station/research/experiments/1059.html

Fleeter, R. (2000). *The Logic of Microspace (The Space Technology Library, Vol. 9)*. El Segundo, California: Microcosm Press.

Fletcher, K. (2009). *Assessment of Cold Welding between Separable Contact Surfaces due to Impact and Fretting under Vacuum*. Noordwijk, The Netherlands: European Space Agency.

Garner, R., & Frazier, S. (2015, Sept 30). *Real Martians: How to Protect Astronauts from Space Radiation on Mars*.

Retrieved from NASA's Goddard Spaceflight Center: https://www.nasa.gov/feature/goddard/real-martians-how-to-protect-astronauts-from-space-radiation-on-mars

Gordon, M. R. (1997, Jul 15). *Mir Commander's Heart Ills Cast Doubt on Repair Effort*. Retrieved from New York Times: http://www.nytimes.com/1997/07/15/world/mir-commander-s-heart-ills-cast-doubt-on-repair-effort.html

Hansen, C. P. (2013). *International Space Station (ISS) EVA Suit High Visibility Close Call*. Washington, D.C.: NASA.

Hersee, E., Hurt, M. T., & Pruzin, S. J. (2000). *International Space Station Malfunction Checklist*. Houston, Texas: NASA Lyndon B. Johnson Space Center.

Jarvis, A. M., McDaniel, R. S., Fitts, M. A., Payne, L. P., & Hurt, M. T. (2001). *International Space Station EVA Checklist*. Houston, Texas: NASA Lyndon B. Johnson Space Center.

Jones, B., & Bryukhanov, N. (2000). *Non-Recoverable Cargo (Trash/Waste)*. Houston, Texas: NASA International Space Station Program Johnson Space Center.

Knapton, S. (2014, Oct 26). *Space may make astronauts infertile, scientists fear*. Retrieved from The Telegraph: http://www.telegraph.co.uk/news/science/space/11188562/Space-may-make-astronauts-infertile-scientists-fear.html

Knapton, S. (2015, May 1). *Mars astronauts could develop dementia on journey to Red Planet*. Retrieved from The Telegraph: http://www.telegraph.co.uk/news/science/space/11576788/Mars-astronauts-could-develop-dementia-on-journey-to-Red-Planet.html

LeClaire, S. (2015, Jan 13). *How Do Astronauts Weigh Themselves in Space?* Retrieved from Air and Space Magazine-

Smithsonian Institution: http://www.airspacemag.com/daily-planet/how-do-astronauts-weigh-themselves-space-180953884/

Loff, S. (2017, Aug 4). *Solar Arrays on the International Space Station*. Retrieved from NASA: https://www.nasa.gov/content/solar-arrays-on-the-international-space-station

Margolis, J. (2015, Mar 15). *40 years and counting: the team behind Voyager's space odyssey*. Retrieved from The Guardian: https://www.theguardian.com/science/2015/mar/15/voyager-1-and-2-space-journey-nasa#img-3

Matty, C. M. (2008, Jun 29). Overview of Long-Term Lithium Hydroxide Storage aboard the International Space Station. *SAE International*, 2008-01-1969. Retrieved from https://doi.org/10.4271/2008-01-1969

McCuaig, K. E., & Houtchens, B. A. (1992). Management of trauma and emergency surgery in space. *Journal of Trauma and Acute Care Surgery*, 610-626.

McNutt Jr, R. L., Andrews, G. B., James, M. V., Gold, R. E., Santo, A. G., Ousler, D. A., . . . Williams, B. D. (2000). *A Realistic Interstellar Explorer*. Laurel, MD: The Johns Hopkins University Applied Physics Laboratory.

Millis PhD, J. P. (2017, Jun 18). *Matter-Antimatter Power on Star Trek*. Retrieved from Thoughtco.: https://www.thoughtco.com/matter-antimatter-power-on-star-trek-3072119

Mission Operations Directorate, Systems Division. (n.d.). *International Space Station Maintenance & Repair Group (MRG) In-Flight Maintenance Book Expedition 1 Flights*. Houston, Texas: NASA Lyndon B. Johnson Space Center.

NASA. (2000). *Inflight Maintenance Intravehicuar Activity Installation/Deinstallation*. NASA.

NASA. (2000). *International Space Station Emergency Operations*. NASA.

NASA. (2001, Nov 2). *Good Vibrations*. Retrieved from NASA Science Beta: https://science.nasa.gov/science-news/science-at-nasa/2001/ast02nov_1/

NASA. (2007, Feb 26). *Grand Theft Pluto: New Horizons Gets a Boost From Jupiter Flyby*. Retrieved from www.NASA.gov: https://www.nasa.gov/mission_pages/newhorizons/news/jupiter_flyby.html

NASA (Director). (8 July 2011 15.29 UTC). *Full Cockpit Launch + Crew audio Last Space Shuttle ♦ STS-135* [Motion Picture].

Okutsu, M., & Longuski, J. M. (2000). Mars Free Retruns Via Gravity Assist. *American Institute of Aeronautics & Astronautic*.

Pultarova, T. (2012, Dec 25). *It's All about People: NASA Psychiatrist Explains Why Space Itself Is Not Detrimental*. Retrieved from Space Safety Magazine: http://www.spacesafetymagazine.com/spaceflight/commercial-spaceflight/its-people-nasas-shrink-explains-space-detrimental-human-mind/

Rahn , D., & Brown , D. (2000). *ZVezda: Cornerstone for Early Human Habitation of the International Space Station*. Washington, D.C.: NASA.

Rogers, W. P. (1986, Jun 9). *Report of the PRESIDENTIAL COMMISSION on the Space Shuttle Challenger Accident*.

Russell, C. (2009). *New Horizons: Reconnaissance of the Pluto-Charon System and the Kuiper Belt*. Los Angeles: Springer.

Sivolella, D. (2016). Life Support Systems of the International Space Station. *Handbook of Life Support Systems for Spacecraft and Extraterrestrial Habitats*, 1-13.

Steigerwald , B. (2006, Apr 14). *New and Improved Antimatter Spaceship for Mars Missions*. Retrieved from NASA Goddard Space Flight Center: https://www.nasa.gov/exploration/home/antimatter_spaceship.html

Tomayko, J. E. (Mar 1988). *Computers in Spaceflight: The NASA Experience*. Wichita, Kansas: Wichita State University.

Van Hooser, K., & Bradley, D. P. (2011). *Space Shuttle Main Engine — The Relentless Pursuit of Improvement*. Long Beach, CA: American Institute of Aeronautics and Astronautics.

Wells, N., Schlesinger, J., & Chemi, E. (2017, Jul 27). *These AI bots are so believable, they get asked out on dates*. Retrieved from CNBC: https://www.cnbc.com/2017/07/27/these-ai-bots-are-so-believable-they-get-asked-out-on-dates.html

Wierks, K. (2017, Feb 17). *Indiana University researcher sending mice to space to study bone healing, help wounded soldiers*. Retrieved from CBS4Indy.com: http://cbs4indy.com/2017/02/17/indiana-university-researcher-sending-mice-to-space-to-study-bone-healing-help-wounded-soldiers/

Williams, D. E. (2007). *International Space Station Temperature and Humidity Control Subsystem Verification for Node 1*. Houston, Texas: NASA, Johnson Space Center. Retrieved from https://ntrs.nasa.gov/archive/nasa/casi.ntrs.nasa.gov/20070018272.pdf

Wolverton, M. (2007, May). *The G Machine: Riding an Atlas into space was a piece of cake compared to pulling 32 Gs on the Johnsville centrifuge.* Retrieved from AIR & SPACE MAGAZINE: http://www.airspacemag.com/history-of-flight/the-g-machine-16799374/?page=2

CPSIA information can be obtained
at www.ICGtesting.com
Printed in the USA
LVOW07s0317071117
555333LV00023B/1226/P

9 781977 718365